Reviews

Outstanding!!

'Michele has a way with words that is raw and brilliant. I can tell she is passionate about her work and puts a lot of thought about every word she writes. I'm a big fan of her work and this book definitely didn't disappoint. I highly recommend this book and any of her work. She is talented with the pen!!!!!'

An image that stuck in my head long after I had finished reading

'This book has five separate short stories, with varying themes and perspectives. I found that the first story was the most harrowing, and stuck with me throughout the book, although all are strong and unique. The "**Drunkface**" story was so well written though, I have not seen many short stories so quickly and fully immerse the reader, nor be as personal and hard hitting.'

Goodness! What a full-on read

'This book would be ideal to dip into - I read it in one sitting (because I just couldn't put it down) and I struggled to re-adjust the voice in my head, between stories. Absolutely not a criticism of the book. Each story is completely separate and stand alone - all quite dark as the body count increases. There is something quite Kafkaesque about the style, especially **Blood Moon** and **The Needling** (my favourites). Glad I picked up this book, but should have read one story per day!'

A breath of fresh air

'So many story collections fall short and are forgotten after your eyes pass over the last period. Not with **Drunkface**.'

Almost Kafkaesque

'Goodness! What a full-on read. This book would be ideal to dip into - I read it in one sitting (because I just couldn't put it down) and I struggled to re-adjust the voice in my head, between stories. Absolutely not a criticism of the book.'

Compelling prose

'This is the second compilation of stories I have read from this author and I was certainly glad I did. Each one is written with absolute skill, the narrative drawing the reader into each scene while leaving no choice than to keep turning the pages.'

Gripping fantastically written fiction that is too close to the truth

'This is the second book of short stories I've read by this author. In some way, I would frame these in a horror genre, in that they are pieces of fiction that are a slither from reality but contain malevolent undertones.'

DRUNKFACE

M. HENNINGHAM

First published in the UK in 2010

Michele Henningham

For my grandparents who are like guardian angels with hearts of gold. Their love wraps around me, shielding me from life's storms with unwavering protection.

About the Author

M. Henningham is a published author who won the 2014 inaugural Bonnie Greer OBE Stories to Read Aloud Competition. She was also published in What Lies Beneath — A Collection of Short Stories from the Kingston Writing School. Selected by Hilary Mantel and Bonnie Greer, OBE. Michele's writing screenplays and collections of short stories that are thrillers with a twist or two. Kingston University produced 'Off the Page', which features her Unscrupulous Pigs. Michele also took part in a series of workshops at Kingston Writing School and read some of her stories at Kingston University, in the Rose theatre, Ram Jam in Kingston, and the Star of Kings, London. Michele received a highly commended for a short story in Writers' Forum and was long-listed by the Fish Short Story Prize, 2015.

INTRODUCTION

I don't have a particular fondness for introductions; anyway, I would like to shed light on the inspirations behind the stories in this collection. To begin with, there's no specific theme or rationale for the content; instead, these stories stem from triggers that sparked my imagination. It just happened that the issues explored within them captivated me enough to weave them into narratives.

I'm consistently fascinated by the idea that readers often experience intense emotions as if the characters were real people. However, some of these stories originated from images and memes, while others sprouted from observations jotted down hastily in a notepad upon my return from a Christmas holiday in the sun. While seated on the plane, awaiting take-off, I observed both the seated passengers and those walking down the aisle, envisioning the possible stories unfolding in their lives. One thought led to another, and before I knew it, I found myself scribbling away like a mad scientist.

Consequently, I landed in London with usable drafts that I read and developed in my short story workshop in Wimbledon. Several stories in this collection are written in the first person, allowing the reader to take a seat in the story's front row. This approach is beneficial as it establishes credibility by creating a personal connection with the audience who can relate to the characters. Another advantage of writing in the first person is that it enables you to capture the character's unique way of speaking. Londoners, in particular, have a distinct way of expressing themselves, which might be perceived as unconventional English by those from other countries, but it isn't incorrect.

This manner of speaking is scattered throughout the collection and is especially pronounced in **"The Great Rocco**," where we follow the adventures of the self-assured protagonist who communicates in the distinctive dialect of English known as Cockney, closely associated with working-class London over the years. Cockney speakers also employ Cockney rhyming slang, a unique linguistic tradition that adds another layer of authenticity to the narrative. Some words may appear nonsensical, but individuals who have grown up in London are more likely to understand their meanings. However, nothing is lost, as Google can be a helpful companion for Cockney translation!

Be warned, these stories are incredibly potent, and once read, they will not be easily forgotten!
Enjoy!

Contents

Drunkface

Paige looks like that man with a patch in Pirates of the Caribbean. Oh God, please don't make 'em come no more. I poke my fingers in my eyes to stop the tears, but I can't. They fall quickly, and my nose runs. Snot hangs in the air like a bungee but doesn't go back up like a bungee does. My heart's beating hard, my hands shake. I shouldn't look, but I'm gonna watch 'til I can't see 'em no more. The blinds don't go up, so I have to get under them 'cause the social worker told Drunkface to cut the strings off to make it safe for me. While Mum and Dad wait for Paige, I watch and snort as he catches up with 'em, and they laugh and run along like they used to do with me. Paige looks scared but laughs really loud. She's about four now with skin like a honey colour, frizzy ginger hair down her back, and a squinty green eye like a cat. She screams her head off, runs away from Mum, and then grabs Dad around the knees.

He was always coming and going 'cause he's a busy businessman. One night, I crept downstairs, and he was in a holey vest and shorts, but Mum and some women were sitting naked in the living room with loads of little bags with skeleton heads on them and heaps of balloons on the table. Sweat dripped down Dad's face, and he didn't wipe it. Then, not long after that, the police took him, and we didn't see him for a long time. Mum told me he had gone away, and she couldn't stop crying. I was playing on my Nintendo one day in my room, and I heard her, so I came out and asked what was wrong. She said nothing, but later, she was on the phone to Dad, saying she'd had enough.

I didn't understand what she'd had enough of. Later, she came in, picked me up, and told me she had a surprise for me. I was so confused and scared 'cause she cried hard on my shoulder. In minutes, she'd filled my rucksack and zipped up my jacket.

We got off the train and went into this massive grey building that she said belonged to the government. I didn't even know what that was or why we were going there. Inside, she took a ticket from a machine and gave it to me. While we sat, she kept staring at me, stroking my hair. When they called our number, we went into a little corner thing with a window. Mum told the woman with the black scarf she couldn't deal with me anymore. I put my head in my hands and just cried and cried. When the man tried to take me, my fingers were claws when they pulled me off Mum. She just turned around and walked out, didn't even look back for me.

The people called Nanny, who wasn't Drunkface then, she went all bonkers and took me out, telling me Mum would take me back after she settled down with Paige. It wasn't long after moving in with Nanny that she started reminding me of the ugly troll under the bridge in 'The Three Billy Goats Gruff.' It was my favourite story, too.

Me and Paige play in the park when Drunkface says I've been good. But even when I'm good, she says I've been bad. That makes me be bad. Very bad! But the little fire wasn't my fault, nor were the red bite marks or the patch thing.

Now, about the patch thing. I swear I never planned it; it just happened. Cameron and me were in the playground, and we found this bit of plastic with a sharp, pointy bit on the end. He got me up against the wall, jacking me. You know, like a real gangster. Miss come by with the bell, and we had to line up, so I grabbed it and shoved it in my pocket.

When Drunkface said we could go to the park, I grabbed my coat, and as we crossed the road, I stuck my hand in my pocket and felt it. At first, I had no idea what it was 'til the tip poked my finger, and then I 'membered.

While chasing Paige, Drunkface was sitting on a bench munching yellow flowers and drinking from a can of White Lightning. Paige ran around the back of the shed, where some kids were thumb-blowing. She laughed her head off, but when she turned and saw the look on my face, she started screaming, and then she started teasing me, just teasing me—her mouth all in a circle.

"I'll tell mummy that you scared me."

I was like, "She's my mum, too, you know!"

Paige started making a racket. "She din't want you, cos you a BADEGG."

That really hurt. Why should Mum want Paige and not me? I came first. Then the tears come, so I put my hand in my pocket for a tissue. Paige was going on and on and on. I 'membered Cameron and pulled out the pointy thing. Paige tried to get to Drunkface by running past me, but I blocked her and stuck it out, and it went in her eye. Yes, it was a horrible thing to do, but I can't do anything about it.

Why can't I be with 'em? It's like they don't care about me no more. Mum told Drunkface she'd come to see me after school. And she comes for a bit, and things are great. She even come with Dad today. But sometimes weeks go by, and I don't see any of 'em. When that happens, I cry a lot, but only when Drunkface lets me go to bed. I don't want her to see me 'cause she'll only get mad and do something. She says I can't be with 'em 'cause of what I did to Paige's eye. Sometimes I have drowning dreams where I wake an' the bed's wet. Once, I tried to hide the sheets, and Drunkface caught me. She gave me such a thump and sent me right back to sleep in the wet patch.

Drunkface rows so much with Mum and Dad, and it scares me 'cause they scream and shout a lot. I hide under the covers with my hands over my ears. Every shout makes my heart beat faster. I keep my hands over my ears and stay still in bed.

When my fingers go stiff, and I can't straighten them, I take 'em off. The place is so quiet.

Drunkface told anyone who'd listen I wasn't well. When people asked what she meant, she tapped the side of her head with her finger. She spoke with my social worker, and they sent me to see Dr. Beckford. I talked about Mum, Dad, Paige, Drunkface, my dreams, and how much I thought about death. I even showed her how I strangle myself when I get things wrong. When I finished, Dr. Beckford picked at her eyelashes like something was in her eye. Minutes later, she sniffed, picked a crumpled tissue from her sleeve and wiped her nose. She made me talk about my feelings by drawing pictures and then asked me to talk about one of 'em. I had to tell her it was a hangman. She looked at me like I said a swear word. Then it was like she wanted to touch or hug me, but she didn't. I wanted to hug her 'cause I felt sorry for her. I couldn't understand why my picture made her so sad.

Paige sees a kid with a Crunchie and wants it. Dad grabs her hand, but she sits on the road and cries her eyes out. She does that at school, too.

At school, they worried about me. Sometimes, I hid when it was P.E. 'cause of the bruises. One day, Miss Ward asked Drunkface about 'em, and she told 'em I was a clumsy kid. When we got home, she let me have it 'cause *they* asked questions. I swore to her I didn't tell 'em anything. A lot of times, Drunkface played wrong and strong about not paying for school dinners 'cause she said they had worked it out wrong. Two weeks ago, I stole a jar of strawberry jam from the shops and took it to school. At lunchtime, I hid in the cloakroom and stuffed my face. Miranda came in, saw it smeared all over my mouth, and snitched. Mrs. Kern came, got me, and took me to the hall for school dinners. I pretended I didn't want seconds, but Mrs. Starr was my angel; she made sure I had more than enough.

A pink ice cream van's coming. Paige screams and points. I'm sweating like a pig. Where was I? Yeah, I kick off big-time at school.

I've even carved my name into the time-out corner, as I pretty much live there. I bite my nails and make them bleed whenever my teacher has to talk to Drunkface 'cause she'll lose it, and I'll get it. I have to speak to her like she's deaf. Only a little bit of what I'm saying goes in when her eyes are foggy.

They've reached the ice cream van. Dad looks round, takes something out of his pocket, and passes it to a BMW man with the roof off. He opens his wallet and gives Dad some money. Mum bends to give Paige a ninety-nine that looks far too big. She bites the flake sticking out of it, and chocolate chunks fall. I try to remember what it tastes like as I press my nose against the window. It's pinchy hot. Last night, the T.V. man said something about it being the hottest summer and something about a record. What's a record? Ice cream drips all down Paige's hand. Mum takes it, licks a lot, wraps tissue round it, and gives it back. Paige's crying. Mum bends and kisses her on the head. Paige smiles at Mum. Did Mum used to look at me like that? I think I'm gonna puke. This happens a lot after I've seen 'em.

When I look again, they're far away. I lift my arms to wipe my face, and I smell Mum. The tears come as I sit in the corner.
From the living room, Drunkface sings badly:

"Ya my sunshine, my only sunshine. Ya make me happy… when skies are grey…"

Then she flippety-flops down the corridor.

"C'mon, Pax," she says, her face all shiny. She grabs and shakes me, knocking one of the flying ducks off the wall.

"What's the matter?" she says, blinking. "Look what I've done for ya! Why the tears?"

"Nanny–"

"Paxton, they don't want ya – get that into ya *thick* skull!"

"But Dad said he's coming back for me. He promised."

"Yeah, sure! Just wait!"

"I want my Mum and Dad," I whisper.

"They don't act like parents. I do." Her spit hits the bottom bit of my eye. I want to wipe it, but a long hair on the end of her nose nearly touches mine. I move my head.

"Why d'ya do this to me, ya little shit?"
For a moment, Drunkface's spit burns my eye. I just stare at the carpet, trying not to blink. Gazing at the pattern under the dirt, I can't work out what colour it used to be. Was I even born when it was new?

"Why?" Drunkface says, "D'ya want to drive me mad?" Suddenly, it feels like ants are crawling on my head. She slaps me.
KA-POW!!!!!!
I think of Batman and shake it off like they do in the movies. I stare at her—my cheek burns.

"I didn't do nothing," I whisper.

"C'mon, ya ungrateful bastard."

She flippety-flops back to the living room, sits down, and lights a cigarette.

Slowly, I go into the room. Drunkface sucks hard on the cigarette before resting it on the side of the ashtray. Then, after she blows out the smoke, her face crunches up like a crybaby,

"I'm so sorry. So sorry."
She grabs me like I'm about to fall, then squishes me against her. She's like, "Please forgive me?" I try not to breathe 'cause when I do, it's like I'm drowning in smoke under her boobs. She coughs, and it sounds like when you pop those fat plastic bubbles in cardboard boxes. Closing my eyes, I pray she lets go. Her massive tears plop on my head. She reaches over me to pull off another can of cider.

"Y'know I love ya, don't ya?"

I can't say nothing.

"Y'know, right?"

"Hmmmmm," I whisper.

"Them two can't even take care of themselves!"

Drunkface takes a long gulp from the can, so I shoot to my feet and run back to the window. There's no sign of Dad, Mum, or Paige but two kids chewing gum and playing footy in the road.

I shut my eyes and pretend Dad's next to me. Then, I feel hands holding me, lifting me to my feet. My heart does a crazy flip. Maybe he's back. But it's only you know who.

"Don't worry," Drunkface says, smiling down at me. I keep my teary eyes glued to the floor.

"Aww, what's brought this on again?" Not waiting for an answer, she puts her arms round me and takes me back into the living room.

"No one ca-ha-hares."

"Ya got me." She looks as if she's seeing me for the first time. I glance up, and tears mixed with snot trickle down my face.

"I wish my Daddy would come."

"C'mon," Drunkface says, pulling me onto the sofa. She forces my head down into her lap. It's like lying on twigs. Her eyes bulge, sweat runs down her face, and her nose is full of tiny holes. I try not to look at her bald bits, so turn to lie on my side. I swallow and clear my throat.

"When're they gonna take me back, Nanny?" She drags her hand across my head, then gulps cider, comes to the bottom, and slurps long and hard.

"Give them time, son."

But I know it's not about time. Drunkface drags her hand across my head for a bit and, thank God, drops off and soon snores. She shakes a little as I move her hand but doesn't wake. I kick one of her black cans with a big red K on it, and it rolls, dribbling onto the carpet. I go into the kitchen and take the blind's string out of the drawer.

Climbing the stairs, I see my face in the mirror, between the three ugly flying ducks on the wall. I hate them as much as I hate Drunkface.

The splotchy red mark on my cheek reminds me of a hand painting I did in Year 2 with Miss Osborne. I was ever so proud of it and wanted Mum to be proud of me, too. I couldn't wait to give it to her when she came to pick me up after school. I had never seen a more beautiful smile than the one on her face. Later, after dinner, I was so helpful, clearing the table and scraping the plates, and saw my painting under gunk in the bin. Maybe she didn't really like it after all.

As I'm just about to go into my room, I hear the doorbell ring; it makes me jump. I run to the window.

"It's Dad, it's really Dad!"

I turn around and go flying downstairs, two at a time.

Insane Reality

The white envelope fluttered to the carpet, and a pulsing white rage washed over Wilma as she digested the accusing red capitals. It was less than a second, maybe half a second, but it changed everything. She bolted out of the house — without locking the door — and hit the high road. As Dudley ambled out of the betting shop, they collided. Their eyes locked; he clutched his chest and dropped dead right there in the street.

In twelve years, he'd run up debts she knew nothing about. What was worse, he'd sunk their retirement plan. After a while, Wilma regained the plot — or so she thought – and took out loans. With the bills that kept coming, the funeral director's cost, coffin, and the rest, it rocked her to the core. She wanted to rip the lid off Dudley's coffin, kill him again, and die too.

It seemed that time slipped away from Wilma, and the place was a royal mess. Cobwebs in the living room window were ginormous; it looked like spiders had taken over the mortgage. All of the shelves bulged, everywhere on every surface sat things – hundreds of things. Next door's Hyacinth was telling tales again, and that's why Frank called. She told him the garden brimmed with all kinds of junk and that Wilma had been staring at walls and screaming the place down at night. She had to act like the old Wilma, the one shown the utmost respect at Woodward Primary. The one suited and booted to a precision only mastered by Kenley's of Knightsbridge. Digging a manky flannel from under rags and sheet music, Wilma picked up half a litre bottle of Evian and giggled:

"Pure and natural from the Alps. A perfect balance of minerals. Mother nature's recipe. Well, we'll see about that."

Wilma opened the bottle and sniffed the water. She took two big gulps before grabbing the flannel, dousing it with water, and then popping it in the microwave. When it pinged, Wilma wiped her body from head to toe and got dressed. Afterwards, she glanced in the mirror, put on a dab of lavender lipstick, and powdered her nose. When satisfied she was finished, she gave herself the once-over. There was no wisp of hair out of place, nor run in her Wolford's.

After gulping Vodka from a tumbler, she yanked a jacket from a pile of clothing mixed with trash and collectibles and swung it over her shoulders. As she took another slug, the doorbell rang. Wilma put the tumbler down, causing Vodka to spill over her hand. She slurped between the index finger and thumb and wiped her hand on her skirt. Wilma crunched the stray extra-strong mints she found in her pocket, glanced in the mirror, and took several deep breaths before opening the door. The Bagua mirror swayed to and fro as her baby, her Frank, stood there. She moved forward, blocking him from coming in. He sighed, turned, and they got into the car.

It was late when they arrived at Starbucks, and most of the rush-hour crowd had gone. They sat outside with cappuccinos.

"You haven't let me in since Dad died."

"Sometimes... I just need to get out."

"Hyacinth says... you're a fire hazard... and the bawling."

"Well, the old cow needs to mind her own damn business."

"Mum, you could set fire to the whole neighbourhood."

"Just want to be... alone..."

"What're you on about?"

"Something's... in... there," she whispered as if the something could hear.

"I can get you help."

"Help?"

"Yes, professional."

"Don't say that, Frankie. They'll lock me up."

"No, they won't."

"You're only saying that 'cause you and your floozy want the house," she sneered.

Frank's heart stopped. "I don't know what you're talking about! Mum, we want you to get well... be well."

Wilma scratched a bump under her ear.

"Ah, drink up and take me home!"

Frank pulled up in the drive. Wilma yanked off her seatbelt and zipped out of the car like she'd left something on the stove. She opened the front door before Frank had even switched off the engine. Wilma stopped to survey the walls. Her eyes were fixed on a point way over her head, then darted like a bead on a moving target. Frank tugged the key and got out of the car; he shook his head in consternation and stood behind Wilma with his eyes fixed on the window panes, trying to see what she saw. Then, seeing her absorbed, he slipped past and entered the house.

Meanwhile, Wilma had taken bits of wool from her bag and started plugging holes and cracks. Her face showed a mixture of confusion and amazement. Afterwards, she filled the ones in the grate and behind the plumbing pipes. By the time she reached the window, a flabbergasted Frank was in the living room.

"FRANK. FRANK..." she shouted, thrusting open the door.

"OH-MY-GOD ..." he replied, taking in the surroundings.

"This is unbearable; they're absolutely everywhere, Frankie."

"You've got stuff all the way to the damn ceiling, Mum."

"Frank, please don't..."

"Rotten orange, apple peel, and banana skins need to be in the bin, not on the mantelpiece!"

"Don't they make the place smell – potpourri-ish?"

"You don't even like pepper," he said, scrutinising the dark, brown, oval shapes.

"But your Dad does."

"Dad? Clean this mess and stop with the visions, Mum."

"They're not visions; they're real."

"Dead rats, for Chrissakes…"

"Hyacinth's cat must have…"

"Mum, keep taking the tablets, or you know what'll happen." With that, Wilma sobbed. Frank put his arms around her, then staggered with her through the rubbish tunnels into her bedroom. He helped her to undress, and then he cleared a path for her to the single bed in the corner. As he drew back the sheets and blanket, Frank wrinkled his nose at the odour that rose up to greet him. Wilma wriggled in. She lay there looking like a shrunken Peruvian head under a window frame thick with damp. After a while, Frank started to say something, but he remained silent. He left to tidy up and open windows. As soon as he'd gone, the bedsprings creaked as Wilma leaned out of bed, found the tumbler, and took a healthy slug of Vodka before she fell asleep. It was well after midnight when he returned, but she howled the minute he closed the door. Frank reappeared in the doorway.

"They're going to kill me, Frank," Wilma whispered.

"There is no THEY!" Frank declared.

"I crushed them 'til the cracking didn't bother me; that's why…"

"Right, that's it! I'm going to call them in the morning."

"Don't, Frankie."

"I've seen them… in the trees…"

"It's all in your mind, Mum."

"Last night, they came out of the vent, and when I tried to get them, a couple crawled over my foot."

"Mum, this didn't happen when you were on the tablets."

"Stop with bloody tablets, will you? I wish you'd listen to me!"

"You used to run through here with gloves that stayed white when you finished with them. What's happened?"

"What do you mean by that?"

"I don't know Mum. I just don't know."

Frank took out his handkerchief, folded it repeatedly, and wiped his lips.

"But your Dad was never bloody satisfied, was he?"
Frank perched at the foot of the bed. "I keep smelling something, Mum..." he said, wrinkling his nose.

"Smell?"

"Hmmm, like Alcolado."

"Yeah, sometimes it puts them off."

"Sure... sure."

"They come at night," Wilma said, clutching the blanket.

"Belief kills, and belief cures, Mum," Frank told her, scratching his chin.

"It's true, Frankie."
Wilma was at the end of her rope, red-rimmed eyes, lips blue, and all a quiver. For a moment, she looked startled as if aroused from a deep sleep.

Frank massaged a spiny foot through the blanket.

"Who's trying to kill you, Mum?"

"Roaches..."

"Don't be silly."

"White..."

"There are *no* white ones!"

"I've seen..."

"C-can't keep going through this... 'cause..." Frank carried on, let go of her foot, and put his head in his palms. Yes, the place was full of crap and smelled of the dead, and she had shown him what she thought were droppings, but he was sure it was dirt.

"All in your head," he said, still with head in his hands. Frank could not say much else. He knew there was little point. More than that, he wanted to go and never return, but he couldn't leave his mother. Frank folded his handkerchief repeatedly and wiped his lips with it. After he put it in his breast pocket, he studied Wilma as she stared from one corner of the room to the other. It was almost as if watching her observe an invisible tennis match. Frank was really confused to say the least.

For a long time, Frank lay awake on the sofa, waiting. It was between three and four am when the second scream came. Frank clambered over stacks and stacks of stuff – some things caked in dust but brand new in taped boxes – balanced on top of clusters of black bin bags. He shot into Wilma's room to see her with her lips peeled back from gritted teeth. She stared at him with a blank expression and scratched at the bump under her ear. Wilma said nothing as blood trickled down the side of her neck. Frank could not believe his eyes. He quickly cleaned her up, closed the door, and stood there with his hand on the doorknob for the longest time. In the morning, Wilma emerged from her nest, embarrassed and looking like someone on the brink of madness.

"You ready to see Dr. Ellman?" Frank asked.

"Nowt wrong with me," Wilma snapped.

Frank thought he had her. "It's every bloody night, Mum," he said, slamming the door.

That afternoon, Wilma nursed the tumbler while Frank took another trip to the shops. One of the things she'd asked him to get knocked him for a six – Baking soda — but he didn't want to push. He just wanted peace, and he also reasoned that he'd never eat another bite from her anyway. He found Wilma with a stick in one hand and a torch in the other on his return. She gasped, stumbling downstairs towards the cellar. For a moment, she stopped, her shoulders shaking with silent laughter.

"Come and see, Frankie."

Frank shuddered, put on a fake smile, and said, "Crown jewels, I hope."

Without too much interest, he unlocked his phone and descended into the clutter. Dark and damp filled the cellar, but there was another more rancid stench.

Frank retched.

"Frankie, get them!"

"No, thank you!"

Frank cupped his mouth and watched his mother stagger around. His eyes widened as she crouched and stabbed at the floor.

"Generations..." she said, shivering. Frank swallowed for a moment, forcing down the lump in his throat and looked away. He shuddered after yet another bout of nausea and mopped sweat on his brow.

"Look, love," Wilma said.
Frank's face was tense, and his eyes narrowed as if he was expecting a punch.

"Mum, you can't do that," he said in the voice of one who sees another levitating.

"You can't..."

"See," Wilma whispered, "See."
For a minute, Frank was sure he was about to vomit, but it passed. He gawked at a writhing wet patch.

"What did you do, Mum?"

"Baking soda."

"What for?"

"You'll see."

"Hmmm..."

"I got... trapped them. I put a few on a tray with the Baking soda, and all their bits bubbled out."

"You did *what*?"

"Went to get a drink of... water, and when I returned, their legs were in the air."

"Mum, how on earth could you?"

"Added bleach... you know, that one-pound stuff... poured it on some of them, and they got really puffy and juice..."

"Stop. Don't want to hear any more of this madness!"

"It's kill or be killed, Frankie!"

"Mum, there's nothing there."

"Ah, but there was," Wilma said.

"I..." Actually, it stumped Frank. "I think you need help," he said, hoping for an end to it.

For a moment, he stared blankly. A stabbing pain rose from behind his ear. Overcome with revulsion, he prised the stick out of Wilma's hand, flung it in a corner, then took her by the elbow and guided her upstairs.

"You're behaving very oddly," Frank said finally. "Let's get your tabs... I'll wait 'til they start working."

"Don't need any damn tablets." she sneered.

"You'll hurt yourself." Frank shook a few tablets out and gave them to Wilma.

She sat on the bed and pretended to swallow.

"Yes, you'd like that!"

Without hesitation, he turned and put the rest of the tablets in the cupboard; Wilma hid hers in the pillowcase. She pulled the blanket under her chin, her knuckles white in the light between the window's blackened curtains. Ten minutes later, she seemed to be asleep. Frank paused inside the door, his hand on the doorknob, listening. After Wilma turned on the pillow and settled, he tiptoed to her bedside and gaped. Her skin was waxy, cool, but mottled. Sunken grooves framed her eyes. What happened to her? Wilma opened a blood-shot eye and stared back. A tear trickled from the corner of Frank's eye as he forced a smile. He'd never seen her look like that before.

"No worries. Sleep, Mumsy." His eyes were wide, and he put his finger to his lips.

As Wilma closed her eyes and drifted, Frank scanned the room. Finding nothing, he tiptoed downstairs, but something rustled in the corner of Wilma's bedroom. As she dropped off, part of her thoughts was on Frank's face, and the other was on the roaches in her dream. She knew their rain-like whisper. She was escaping, but they were close. Wilma sat bolt upright in bed. Suddenly, she felt the hooks of claws as they dug into her. Then they were gnawing at her eyes, ears, mouth. She opened her mouth to yell, then stopped. Her breath stuck behind a ball of pressure. Her eyes were saucers, pupils larger than life.

"Fra..." she mouthed.

She groped at her throat. Frank charged through the door, noting the rise and fall of Wilma's chest.

"Mum! What's wrong? What on earth?!"

As Wilma's complexion paled, the hairs on Frank's head bristled. His distress almost unbearable; he whipped out his mobile phone and dialled for an ambulance. Then, he wiped his forehead and lips with his handkerchief.

Frank paced as paramedics cleared piles of hoarded rubbish, countless flatpack cardboard boxes, plastic and glass bottles, and heaps of magazines and newspapers. The paramedics placed Wilma on a stretcher and tightened the straps. Frank folded his handkerchief repeatedly and wiped his lips. As soon as he popped it into his breast pocket, Wilma reached out and gripped his fingers until his hand ached and turned purple. When Frank bent over to kiss his mother's forehead, a white blur shot from the corner of Wilma's lips, skittered around the back of Frank's neck and disappeared.

Blood Moon

Something's bothering Toby because he wriggles like a slick bare-knuckle fighter in my arms. I have to duck and dive to stop him from clobbering me on the nose. It's as if he can't keep still, no matter what I do. Quickly wiping my brow, I force him into his seat, secure the seatbelt, and yank the strap. He screams as if I'm trying to murder him, stiffening with his legs straight out. Then comes the pièce de résistance–his fifty miles per hour scissor kicks.

"No-o-o-o-o!"
I clamp his thigh with a vice-like grip.

"Mum used to freak out when it was a blood moon. She said it was a rare event and that the sun would turn into darkness and the moon into blood before the great and terrible day of the Lord comes—"

"Not so hard," Pete says, leaning over to examine my handiwork. Toby's shocked into silence when the plane sways violently as it approaches the runway.

"You're so understanding when the shoe is on the other foot, huh?"

"But," says Pete, "at least I try."

"Whatever," I say, stroking Toby's head, "action speaks louder than words, Pete."
Pete rolls his eyes and groans.

"Give him here, then."

"He's fine where he is, thanks!"
Pete looks at me with pain in his eyes.

"Why do you *hate* him so much?"

"No, no, it's not *hate*. You don't seem to understand."

Pete opens his mouth to speak but closes it again; his shoulders droop, and he sighs loudly. Toby makes a racket as the plane takes off, and he's pressed against the back of his seat, a look of utter bewilderment crossing his scrunched face.

"No-o-o-o-!" From Toby again, the word is long and drawn out. "No-o-o-o-o-o-o!"

It's about all he can say that we understand. I take the opportunity to slip a boiled sweet into his mouth, which he sucks for dear life. There's a haggard blonde in front with an old man. I can't work out if he's the husband, father, lover, brother, or friend. I catch snatches of her badgering him to put his coat on because the air-con will make him sick. Her voice drops to a whisper, undoubtedly discussing us. Toby loses his mind as the plane ascends into a flawless blue sky. The haggard blonde scowls; her whole face goes into concertina mode, and she rolls her eyes. I secretly hope those eyes tumble to the floor, giving me the chance to stomp them. That'll teach her. I wish people would try to understand; they're always whispering. I'm so over the *whispering*. They think I can't hear them, but I hear every word. Toby lets out a yelp and squirms, attempting to free himself from the seatbelt. My face flushes; I can't seem to calm him down. Maybe he's just tired. Toby sucks in a loud breath, then exhales.

"No-o-o-o-o-o-o!"

Maybe his ears have popped, but he can't say. Pete whispers some kind of blackmail to get him to be quiet. When that doesn't work, he sings in his ear, "Where are you going, Toby boy, Toby boy, where are you going, charming Toby…"

Finally, without rhyme or reason, Toby settles and drums his feet as if he's in the business of record-making. The childless couple behind tut and moan. After singing until his tongue turns pebble-dry, Pete's forced to stop. Toby opens his mouth wider than I thought possible for a child his size and roars in his face like the ferocious MGM lion. My stomach does hoops. Anyone would think Toby's been birthed by pure evil.

Pete releases the seatbelt and tries to pick him up, but he grapples like Tyson, giving him a swift bop on the nose. Blood splashes everywhere, so Pete hands Toby back to me. He always passes him back to me. I lay Toby's head on my chest, and he's still. I think it's the rhythm of my heartbeat. I glance over at Pete, who holds his head straight as he whips tissue after tissue out of the air-hostesses hands and then stuffs balls of tissue up his nose to stop the blood. I can't help but smirk. Pete gazes at me for a moment with a hurt look in his eyes. I press my face close to Toby's head and inhale his natural sweetness.

When Toby was much younger, it was a battle to get him to sleep. I would lie on the bed, prop him on my chest, and he'd be off in no time. I can't see his face, but he's dead calm. I look over at Pete, and he clenches his hands together, tilting his head to let me know it's working. My shoulders sag, and I relax.

For the first time since we boarded the plane, we actually talked. However, we avoid discussing therapy, moods, insomnia, or hallucinations. Instead, we focused on the beautiful holiday, the balmy weather, the time in the car when the moon was red and humongous, and the places we visited. We also talked about how Toby played in the pool with his new friend, Romeo, and his massive inflatables and how they screamed with delight, chasing them when the wind kept blowing them away. Although the conversation is a little stilted in places, I feel, at least, it's a step in the right direction.

The haggard blonde nods off and snores like a freight train. Beside her, the old man wheezes like he's struggling to breathe. The "Hottest Mum of the Year" award goes to a blonde, bubbly sort who frogmarches her son down the aisle. He looks the same age as Toby. I sit up straight, being careful not to disturb him. I really need to see the boy's face. I must see it. It's funny, but I've always thought that children's faces say so much about them. He is so handsome, a handsome little feller.

The little boy's face is like something Leonardo da Vinci painted. He's called Jackson. No doubt he'll grow up handsome, break hearts, be famous, and overachieve. Toby's hair tickles my chin, and as I flatten it with my hand, I realise I'll have no ticker-tape or Olympic moments to celebrate. He'll never be a Jackson. That's all I ever wanted.

See, I yearned for a baby – Pete yearned too. Do you know what it is like to want? To really want – more than you want to live? The desire becomes so overwhelming that it makes you feel sick with anxiety. The months roll around, and you check the calendar, scheduling routine sex. It's not sex for pleasure at this point; it's sex for the species' survival. So, there's no fifty-shades of anything. Pete's expertise with spreadsheets helps me draw up a timetable of my menstrual cycle. Then he proceeds to ask if I fancy jiggy-jiggy at every opportunity. I mean, I could have been having brain surgery for all he cared. It was like Christmas had come early for him; he could only sleep on his back. I grin and bear the *jiggy-jiggy* even though he fucks as if he is fresh out of the womb. When Pete is finished and has a fag, I lie in bed with my legs in the air, being careful not to spill a drop.

Days later, I consult the mirror and smile because my stomach looks full, as if I am with child. My breasts are bloated, nipples sore, and I feel an intense bout of nausea that actually makes me smile. I even waddle as I board the train for the morning commute. I check my 'Baby on Board' badge and glance around with begging eyes for someone to free up a seat. A kind young man offers, and I take it. As I sit, I think of Pete.

"I've done it! Shot in a good load last night! I could've done it again, too!" he said.

He always marvels at his reproductive juices, and he is pushing fifty, but after all we'd been through, I thought of his spawn more like old wounded soldiers that weren't up to much. I prayed that one of them had enough oomph for the mighty journey to my eggs.

I told God I wanted a baby. Sometimes, with Pete—I love him to death—I thought I had one. Desperation brought us together and told me to lower my standards, as time was not on my side. Pete has a decent job and looks doable on the outside, so I hang on in there. Every month, I pray I'm pregnant, and this goes on despite the fact that deep down inside, something says I'm not, and yet I put myself through it repeatedly. I cried every time the blood came. And boy, did it come. Rivers of blood. The most vibrant red ever—so alive and yet dead as a bunch of dodos. Sometimes, I felt like I was trying to scrape yolk back into an eggshell. My body failed—again.

We press on with the sex thing, and sometimes, after we do it, Pete, who claimed to be teetotal when we met, sits in the living room drinking gallons of Merlot like he has shares in a vineyard. We tried and lost so many times. I had a bottomless lacuna where I needed a baby. Then, one day, we hit the money spot. Boom! We hugged rib to rib and danced to the tune of ecstasy that only we heard. No major morning sickness episodes existed, but some weird cravings took hold. I developed a serious craving for hot Twiglets dipped in peanut butter and yoghurt, and I became Fag Ash Lil every time we went down the pub with me scooping ash out of random ashtrays and smothering my tongue.

Pete seemed to enjoy the taste, too, always thrusting his tongue into my mouth. He embraced the role of the doting father-to-be, placing cushions where I needed them most. He even rubbed my feet despite not being the foot kind of guy. In short, I wanted for nothing. However, as the months passed, unlike some mothers who claimed to enjoy their babies kicking, I didn't. Even then, it felt as if Toby was fighting me. I mentioned the extreme pain to the doctor, and he explained it was natural as the baby's feet and arms were growing stronger. I mean, they were sharp, stabbing pains, like he sat in there prodding with a Stanley knife for goodness sake. I hoped and prayed that I wasn't bringing a serial killer into the world.

When I told Pete, I broke out in a cold sweat when he told me about a case where a new mum nearly died after her unborn baby kicked so hard through the uterus wall into the main abdominal cavity. I mean, she ended up with a torn womb.

I said no when they asked if I wanted to take the screening test. I discussed it with Pete, and we were at loggerheads. He thought it was a good idea, and on most occasions, he was my voice of reason. However, I'd made up my mind that no matter what, I was going to have a baby or die trying. And so, we continued with the plan until finally, it happened.

An interior tidal wave ejected my long-awaited miracle after many hours, and the pain was without definition. I gaped excitedly and brimmed with maternal bliss at our shiny, purplish alien. He was a living, barely breathing stick insect with transparent skin like a little bird. His eyes were bulging but sealed shut, and his mouth was a gaping hole with little bird lips. I could even see his heart beating, a bit like the nose flashing when you hit the sides in a game of Operation.

Nevertheless, he was my legacy and contribution to humanity. After a while, my vagina throbbed when the placenta plopped out like his long-lost twin. Gawping at me, Pete's mouth hung open like he had witnessed Armageddon. Pete and I stared at Toby; then we stared at each other before the midwife rushed him away from us to do checks. It felt like the air had been sucked out of the room when she returned.

"I can understand why you might not want him."

"What!?"

She gazed at the floor for a moment or two, then her eyes flicked upward to meet mine. For a brief second, our eyes locked.

"I'm afraid it looks like he's got Cer—"

"I don't care! Stop!"

"I think you ought to know."

"Stop!"

Needless to say, I didn't care. I couldn't leave him. We couldn't leave him. After we got home, I called and reported the nurse. Pete and I learned how best to cope with Toby through a lot of trial and error.

The first months were okay in getting used to routines and learning what the different cries meant. But it was a different kind of struggle with Toby. Will he want sex? Will I be a doting grandmother one day? Will someone... anyone fancy him, and will countless Instagram models fight for his attention? All of these questions swirl around in my head in the early hours, and I can't help but wonder. But the sad truth is that he will always need me in some way, shape, or form. Long after the point where most kids become independent and mature, my son's neediness will go on indefinitely. Who will take care of him when I can't? Once, in the wee hours, I woke Pete and told him.

"Life's not like veneers. You can't just go out and pick the ones you like. You wanted a baby, and now you got one," he said.

Toby is definitely mine, though; he's got my lopsided smile. People always stare. I know the look well; it's what pity looks like. They're asking all those questions. Surely, before you have the baby, they do tests for defects and complications. I reflect while Toby sleeps. He looks so peaceful. Normal. A normal little boy.

Suddenly, an ungodly odour grips the air, and haggard face wakes up, sniffing like a rat searching for chocolate. The stench is so overpowering that it almost makes me reach for an oxygen mask. I'm sorry, but I was really tempted. I glance at Toby and discreetly pat his bottom to see if it's coming from there, but I'm unsure. I ask Pete to check, and he tries to peek at the sides but can't tell.

"Sweet lord, it stinks of hot shit!" the old bag shouts. She takes a vial of heady and mysterious perfume and dots it behind her ears, screwing up her face, and making it look more and more like old chewing gum.

Then she dabs her wrists and sniffs as if examining the air before putting more on the front of her sweater. As if that is not enough, she pulls up the sweater's neck, covering her nose and mouth. After a long while, the stench disappears. The muscles in Pete's face tighten like Skeletor's as he tests the air. An air hostess makes a sympathetic face and carries on serving refreshments. Maybe Toby needs changing. I'll bathe him when we get home.

The moon looms larger than life in the sky when we leave the airport. Can't say I was scared of it, but like mum, I've definitely bought into the idea that bad things happen during a full moon. Is it due to the moon's gravitational pull on the Earth? It affects tides, so maybe it affects us, too. After all, we are mostly water, aren't we? The wind blows warm, then fresh air. It even smells different. It's as if something's coming. Toby dozes on the way home from the airport. Finally, we get home, and I unpack most of our things.
Grinning, Pete draws me tightly to him.
"I'll just nip down to Costco. Don't bathe Tobe; I'll do it when I get back, all right?" he says. "Don't bathe him. I'll try not to be too long." He kisses me. Surprisingly, it's a warm one.

"And you can call me if you really need to. Just relax and play with Tobe 'til I get back."

He kisses me again and starts down the stairs, moving fast before I can change his mind. I know he'll get supplies and have a quick one at the pub. I go into the bathroom. I forget to ask for chocolate and cranberry juice, so I ran barefoot to the window to catch him. Too late, he drives off into the night. The moon is enormous and has a kind of luminous glow. I pull the blind cord and stand face to face with it before opening the window as wide as it will go. Does the moon have something to share with me? Well, it must be with me as there is no one else around. All of the curtains and blinds are closed down the road, and the lights are all out.

From the living room, Toby moans a thick, muffled sound that I can't make out.

"You're going to be fine, Toby. It's almost bath time."

The moaning turns into a banshee-esque wail. It's like an alarm… a fire alarm. It warns of imminent danger. Anyone who hears it would think a child is seriously hurt or threatened in some way.

"Daddy'll be back in a minute."

The reply is met with, "No-o-o-o-o-o!"

This reminds me of the last time it happened when Pete went to work in Runcorn. The damn memories always come flooding back. I must have blacked out, as I couldn't recall more than just giving Toby his bedtime bath. Sometimes, it was live combat getting him in and equally soul-destroying getting him out. But after all that, he slept well. Maybe all the fighting wore him out. For some reason, Toby didn't play up that much with Pete when it came to bath time. Perhaps it was a father and son thing. But Toby lay under the water that time, and the room got so quiet. It was as if I was also under the water, experiencing such a pleasant floaty feeling. When I realised what I was doing, my hand felt like a boulder pressing him down. He thrashed his arms and legs; I mean, he really fought for his life. The poor little thing was livid red when I pulled him out and put him to bed. Pete said that when he got back, all he remembered was me kneeling on the floor, naked, crying, and swigging from a bottle of his Merlot. He said I was gibbering as if talking to someone, but no one was there. Tenderly, he held me and assured me that it was a natural phase that some mothers went through and that I would get over it.

Meanwhile, Toby throws bits of Lego around the living room. I hear the plastic-hitting-the-wall noises. I run the bath and sing about everything he likes to play with. I make sure there are lots of bubbles, ducks, an action man, SpongeBob, and anything else I can throw in. Toby's little thuds tell me he's climbing the stairs. Then he appears at the door and points as hot clouds rise into the air. I put my hand in the water and come up with a mountain of suds.

Holding it out to him, he smiles and reaches out his hand but doesn't come any closer. He frowns while his mouth hangs slightly open. Toby stares as he stands absolutely still for a few minutes. I speak softly, reassuringly.

"Come on, Tobias, it's nice and warm."

He ignores me and stands by the door, gawping like he doesn't trust me. After a few minutes, one hand clenches and unclenches while the other reaches out. I take hold of his soft, pudgy fingers and pull him closer. I kiss his cheek, smile reassuringly and tell him how the water feels and how SpongeBob wants him to get in the bath. The funny thing is, his expression looks a little like disgust, but a smile appears at the side of his mouth like the sun coming from behind the clouds. He comes to the front of the tub and peeps over as if to verify SpongeBob's invitation. As he reaches for him, his tongue slips out and touches his upper lip in deep concentration. I pick SpongeBob up and smack the water with an almighty splash. I grin as water splashes everywhere, and Toby shuts his eyes.

Frantically, Toby reaches for SpongeBob, who is underneath the bubbles. However, no matter how much I coax, Toby still refuses to get in. After a while, I plain lose it. Patience slips out of my grasp and darts right past me as the desire to hurt rushes to the fore. Toby's pleading eyes search my face. The usual struggle ensues. Yes, he's strong, and yes, he fights harder than ever. There's definitely a competition between the water on the floor and the water in the bath. I quickly drag his t-shirt over his head, pick him up, pop him in, and fill the tub with warm water. Amazed at the bubbles, Toby's little mouth twitches in a smile. I want to wash his hair, so I scoop handfuls of water on his head to get him used to the idea, but he stiffens when I tilt his head. Why? Is it that trust thing again? Moments later, he relaxes, his mocha eyes stare up at me. Then the whispering comes. It's persistent too. Always persistent.

Someone calls my name, "Luna." Just like that. It's tranquil, "Luna."

I can't believe it, there's no one but Toby and me. My tongue is suddenly dry like sandpaper; I turn my head quickly when I hear it again, trying to catch where it's coming from. I freeze when it comes again, "Luna, do it."

I know what it wants. I sob, turn, and cry, "Toby." Then, under my breath, "Please don't make me." Something whispers in my ear, "Do it now." Under the water, Toby stares up at me in disbelief. A torrent of bubbles rushes out of his mouth as he opens it to speak. His lips pull back from his teeth. What is he trying to say? Then he stops twisting and thrashing; his face is filled with fear, and his body relaxes. A sudden silence fills the room; the air is humid and heavy.

Out of nowhere, calloused hands grab my waist and tug at my determined arms. Pete's voice booms, "Luna, what on earth are you doing?!"

He pulls at my shoulders. Buckling to the floor, I close my eyes as my heart pounds against my ribs. Pete rushes Toby into the living room like the proud owner of a prize-winning carp. He lays him on the sofa and dries him gently. Toby splutters and breathes rapidly in between sobs. Anyone would have thought someone was trying to kill him. I imagine what his little face looks like. In minutes, Pete's back. He picks me up like a child and escorts me into the living room. He holds me like he'll never let go and looks over my head. "Please," I say, sobbing into his chest.

"Help me, Pete. I need help. Can't do it anymore. I love him so much, but this is too hard."

"We'll call the doctor in the morning!"

Ignoring him, I say, "Please believe... you know I can't... I didn't mean to hurt him. I don't know what came over me." I stand behind the sofa and marvel at my baby's damp hair, wet eyelashes, and chubby cheeks.

Bending down, I reach for his fist resting against his cheek and pull at his fingers. They are cold—icy cold. For a moment, I feel like my heart is fit to explode out of my chest, but I sigh with relief as Toby's eyelids flutter, and my beloved takes a shuddery breath.

The Needling

When Barbara woke that morning, she knew something major was wrong. She couldn't move without intense pain; her glands were cherry tomatoes, and she felt as if she had turned inside out when she retched. Summoning the energy for a cup of tea, she peeped through the curtains to check all was clear, put on her wraparound sunglasses, and stuck a pale-veined hand through a crack in the door for the milk. To her surprise, the milkman saw and said, "Morning."

She had to return his courtesy from behind the door. When she greeted him, she was startled by her voice. It was like she'd wolfed down forty cigarettes, but she'd given up the dirty habit years ago. Shutting the door, she thanked God he hadn't seen her face, especially the swelling around her eyes or the itchy red rash that spread across her nose. He probably wouldn't recognise her anyway. He was far more used to the polished-Heidi Klum-at-thirty she portrayed.

Something was indeed happening to her. There were lumps everywhere—grisly lumps—and she could not work out what caused them. Then came the ugly, blotchy, red marks on her arm, like hives around the spot where she had the injection. What on earth happened? She had had it before. So, what changed?

As far as she was concerned, nothing changed, and that was the main problem. They had been happily married—with the vintage wedding car, "just married" sign, and cans attached—for years until Alex returned from Saudi Arabia with post-traumatic stress disorder and a constant belittling and horrid commentary directed towards her. He soon resorted to therapy at the bottom of a bottle. Barbara was determined to stick it out and stayed strong to help him through it. Eventually, he started taking medication for depression and gave up drinking. He returned to work in the hospital, and things settled. Before long, Barbara discerned that Alex had made many enemies due to his penchant for young, impressionable nurses. Eventually, his indiscretions became less discreet, and the whispers inevitably returned to her.

Everyone at the hospital knew, and it had become a running joke among the staff. Barbara confronted Alex, but he always made her feel that she was delusional, even paranoid. However, she loved Alex so much that she would put up with his shenanigans as long as he didn't physically leave her. But that's just what he did when he met the 'Caliente' Honey-Lee, who gained notoriety for wearing only underwear under a transparent PPE gown in a male hospital ward. Barbara had left the hospital by then because it had all become too much. When she questioned Alex, he said it was nothing serious, but it didn't seem that way to Barbara. Eventually, Alex moved in with Honey-Lee but swore he would return. It was not long before Barbara relocated to another hospital and met Ed, and they fell in love. Barbara was happier than she'd been in a while, but she couldn't deny her chemistry with Alex.

However, Barbara and Alex argued like rebellious teenagers. It was the same old refrain. She would ask Alex when he was coming back, and, as usual, he replied – soon, adding the caveat that Barbara should leave Ed too if she really loved him as much as she said. Deep down, Alex knew Barbara was absolutely nuts about him.

Alex did everything in his power to stop Barbara's nagging. As a result, they soon both became frustrated with the situation. All was quiet for a couple of months until the night they bumped into each other at the hospital where Barbara worked. Alex just happened to be in the ward, talking to a couple of healthcare workers about PPE, when Barbara interrupted to tell him that a patient was having respiratory problems. Alex, being the good doctor went to administer help and left a message for Barbara at the desk to meet with him for a coffee. At first, it was all above board, and they talked about the crisis of not having enough PPE, and she would place orders at his request. Barbara would find ways around any obstacle to get what Alex wanted, be they financial or otherwise. He was impressed with Barbara's desire to please him that he reached over to peck her cheek. She swivelled her face around, and they ended up kissing on the lips.

Then, because Alex was on call, he enjoyed the thrill of their reunion as Barbara would find empty rooms in the hospital so they could have privacy. In no time, they rendezvoused at least three nights a week. But it was too much too soon, so Alex whittled it down to one, and that's when Barbara hit the off switch on Alex's desire. It had all started to feel like an ever-tightening noose around his neck. His main excuse centred on the demands of the practice, but Barbara knew this was not the case because she'd seen Alex and Honey-Lee out on the town.

There were even times when Alex tried to ignore Barbara, but soon stopped when she turned up unannounced at the practice demanding his attention. Therefore, it became official that Friday night was their night, no matter what happened.

Alex fulfilled Barbara's desires by playing for time while figuring out how to get rid of her for good but keep the house. Sometimes, he would wake in the middle of the night with a new strategy but, after examining it every which way, he saw it was not going to work.

It cost him nothing to set up tea candles, scatter rose petals, and run sweet-smelling baths when she came in from work. Afterwards, he'd lay her down, climb on top of her, and massage her with aromatic oils while her skin was moist before they'd make love. After an epic love-making session, he'd sneak out, leaving a bundle of notes on the nightstand for her to go shopping. It went on like this for months, but the calm was destined not to last.

One day, she resorted to a good old-fashioned needling about their relationship and told him she was exhausted. He wasn't surprised; according to him, her mouth seldom tired. Therefore, they tried vitamin pills and various tonics, herbal remedies, and expensive organic potions from China, but none worked. Further analysis revealed that she was anaemic.

Alex conceived the idea of administering vitamin B injections. So, just before bath time on Friday nights, he would give her an injection. However, the last one was different. Due to unforeseen circumstances, they hadn't even had a chance to settle into their usual rituals, as he was running late, and she was tired. When Barbara heard a car outside, she rushed to the window to check if it was Alex, but it wasn't. Finally, utterly exhausted, she lay on the sofa and struggled to keep her eyes open, but she succumbed to sleep before long. The next thing Barbara could recall was Alex bending over and jabbing her arm with the needle. She could barely keep her eyes open. After injecting, he waited ten seconds for it to diffuse into the tissue and then immediately withdrew the needle. However, after glancing at Barbara to ensure she was still asleep, he massaged the injection site and then sat still for a moment on the edge of the sofa before disappearing. Such actions were not considered acceptable in Alex's profession because it was well-known that they could cause the drug to back up through the subcutaneous tissue.

He called the following day, asking how she felt. It was a question
he had never asked before, which Barbara found strange. However,
she thought it might be his way of showing he had seen the light
after their last argument and decided to be a better man. Barbara
felt reassured that Alex was turning over a new leaf.

Deep down, Alex knew it was all his fault. He kept telling Barbara
he would leave Honey-Lee and move back in with her. But if truth be
told, he didn't like how Barbara lay down like lino for him. Silver-
spooned Honey-Lee had moxie and was Alex's trophy, and he had no
plan or desire to leave her. It was just the unbelievable chemistry
that Barbara and Alex shared, making their sex life electric, and he
just couldn't help saying the right things when he wanted to get
some.

One night, after making love to Honey-Lee in the early hours, he
entered the bathroom, opened the cabinet door, studied its
contents, and then closed it. Staring at his reflection in the mirror,
he sighed and ran his fingers through his hair. 'What on earth have I
become?' he thought. The concoction he had given Barbara rolled
around in his mind, and he felt sick to his stomach. Staying away
was the only thing left for him to do, hoping that he could fade out of
her life like a figure in a sepia photograph.

Time passed, and still, Alex remained out of sight but not out of
Barbara's mind. She called his mobile countless times, and the last
attempt told her that Alex had blocked her. Gripping the phone as if
it were Honey-Lee's neck, Barbara listened as the truth registered in
her brain. Something, indeed, was wrong with the picture. Barbara
wiped away the hot tears that rolled down her cheeks.

Ever resourceful, she coaxed someone at the hospital to obtain
Alex's landline number, but Honey-Lee kept picking up the phone,
and Barbara didn't feel ready to deal with her. That day would come
somewhere in the not too distant future.

Hours later, Barbara pulled up in the battered Ford Fiesta and
parked outside Alex and Honey-Lee's townhouse.

She didn't know why or what she planned; it was just where she ended up. Unseen, she turned off the headlights and sat in the cold, under a blanket of black sky, watching. As there were no curtains or blinds in their large windows, she observed that they were doing far better than the Joneses. Rubbing her stomach, Barbara glimpsed her object of affection stroll past the phone in the hallway, so she quickly dialled the number. Alex doubled back to pick it up.

"Tuckin' your fuckin' tail, Alex?" Barbara paused for a moment, letting her voice take root in his head. He was reticent.

"Oh… ahem… Barbara… mmmm. How've you been?" he cleared his throat as if finishing a fit of coughing.

"Feel… like… death."

"Sorry, love, been so busy. The practice has picked up lately, and there's no end to my day…"

"Where does that leave us, Alex?" she said before he could finish.

"What do you mean?" He stammered. "I told you I'm busy. What do you want me to do?"

"Leaving her, huh? But still bedding the bitch, right?"

"I'm working on it. Be patient," he muttered through his teeth. "That's one thing that irks me about you, Barb; you have no patience. Absolutely none!"

"Haven't been feeling well…"

"What's wrong?"

"Can't talk over the phone, but I'm getting an appointment tomorrow."

"No… don't do that. You'll be all right. I'll have a look," Alex said, talking into the receiver but looking around to see if Honey-Lee was in earshot.

"When, Alex?" Barbara said.

"Soon, Barb. Give me time."

"If you don't come, I will… I will…"

"Tomorrow evening," he whispered.

"Please, I need you."

"Okay, okay. I said I'm coming," he whispered, bending over the phone and urging the conversation to end. Barbara sighed and pushed a clump of hair off her face with the back of her wrist.

The next evening, a tipsy, alcohol-reeking Alex came by as planned, their old magnetism off the charts. Barbara dolled up and dimmed all the lights, especially in her bedroom, leaving it dark except for a sliver of light coming from the living room.

"So, what's the problem?" he asked.

"Come, I've got a little treat for you."

Barbara pulled Alex into her bedroom and pushed him down on the bed. She swiftly undid his belt and buckle, and for a moment, Alex found himself admiring Barbara's old position on her knees, ready to engage enthusiastically between his legs. Taking a breath, Barbara looked up at him, licking her lips. However, as they fumbled, Alex accidentally hit the switch on the bedside lamp. Staring into Barbara's eyes, Alex was abruptly brought back to reality, noticing purple grooves etched around them and a livid red rash across her nose under the makeup. Groaning, he distanced himself, and as quick as a wink, he stood up. "Is that the time?" he mumbled, checking his watch. With all fingers and thumbs, Alex buckled up in record time. Barbara gawped at him, a mix of confusion and frustration evident, "Come on, Alex!"

He reassured her that it would be less than a year before they would be together again. He also claimed to have told Honey-Lee that he didn't love her anymore, emphasising that theirs was purely a functional relationship. Barbara felt she had no choice but to issue a threat.

"If you're messing with me, you'll be sorry. I promise!"

"What do you mean? I wouldn't do that, Barb. I love you!"

"Really, Alex?"

"Really, Barb."

"I kept my end of the bargain. Edward's gone. Now, it's your turn, but I see you're a little bit chicken."

"Don't be silly, Barb. Soon, it'll be just you and me until the bitter end… you and me together forever." And with that, he was gone. Barbara had yet to learn that some people just talked because they had a tongue.

The following night, Barbara lay motionless, staring into the darkness. Her new reality made her feel as if she were awake and yet experiencing a nightmare simultaneously. She mulled things over repeatedly until she tossed and turned before finally falling asleep. The bedroom window hung open, the heating turned off, but Barbara woke up in the early hours drenched and shivering. Her heart thrashed, sweat poured down her face. She just about managed to crawl out of bed to call the doctor for an emergency appointment. Barbara couldn't face driving because her nerves were shot to shreds, so she took the underground.

Upon arriving at the surgery, Barbara sat in the waiting room, pondering her situation and trying to figure out why she felt so bad. She took out her compact for a quick look before her name flashed on the screen. Her cheeks were sunken, and her hair looked stringy. She sat crouched forward, silent, not wanting to be seen. Her version of Heidi Klum had left the building. Barbara jumped out of her seat when the buzzer sounded, and her name appeared on the screen, indicating it was her turn to see the doctor.

Baffled, the doctor wasn't sure what to make of her initially but asked if she was on any medication. She explained that she had only been receiving vitamin B shots from Alex. The doctor seemed relieved but ran a series of tests, and the first thing he confirmed was anaemia and pregnancy. Barbara agonised about making the school run in her forties. She pictured herself standing at the school gates, and people thinking that she was there to drop off or collect her grandchild. Then, Barbara felt insane guilt about the binge-drinking episodes.

The doctor said other tests would take a week, and she should call the surgery for an appointment in eight days.

Ten drawn-out, anxious days passed, and Barbara sat biting her nails down to the quick in the waiting room. What else did the doctor test her for? What effect, if any, would it have on the baby? Barbara's heart pounded when the buzzer sounded and her name flashed on the screen. Her legs had gone to sleep, and she couldn't shake the pins and needles when she stood. Barbara couldn't remember how she made it through the door and to the chair next to the table. The doctor asked her if she had unprotected sex and if she did drugs. Next, he paused, took his glasses off, looked her right in the eyes, and told her she had been infected with hepatitis. Barbara's fairy tale came crashing down around her ears. Her heartbeat stopped for a few seconds. She heard what he said but couldn't process the information. Tears poured down her face while her heart pounded. Shock zipped through her body as if someone punched her in the face. Words escaped her for the longest time, but death was the only one that resounded in her head. Barbara's silent sobs turned into a croaky cry as she leaned back in the chair, shaking uncontrollably, twisting her hands together, moaning.

"He's such a psycho piece of shit!"

The next thing she knew, she was headed home. Then she remembered getting off the tube and finding herself at the end of the line, completely opposite where she needed to be. Barbara was a wreck; she couldn't think straight. She ended up at Terri's, hoping she would know what to do.

Barbara sat at the edge of her seat, arms akimbo, lips tight against her teeth, and animated.

"Fuckin' low-life," she said, wiping her nose with the back of her hand. She smacked one fist against her other palm.

"That dirty fucker did this to me."

Terri looked at Barbara with pure sincerity.

"Don't worry, Barb; you can't let it defeat you. I don't think you can die of that," she said. Barbara took a deep breath and cleared her throat.

"But I'm pregnant, too!"

"Shit!" Terri exclaimed.

Barbara felt heat rising from her chest up to her neck and crawling all over her head.

"All that time doing for him, and look what he's gone and done. What did I do to deserve this, Terri? What?"

Terri shrugged her shoulders.

No, Terri, Barbara thought, suddenly filled with rage. I didn't bargain for any of this. I did everything and anything for him... I mean, I slaved and starved to build his fucking practice, and this is my reward?! He's not going to get away with this. I poured so much into our relationship all these years, and he goes and gives me a death sentence. That's what it is! A death sentence. I warned him!

"Yeah, Terri, you're right." As she talked, Barbara's hand knocked her bag off the nest of tables, tossing out her purse's contents.

Terri pointed at a vial of blood.

"What's that? Is it yours?"

"Yeah, no... nothing, it's mine."

Terri didn't ask any more questions; she could see that Barbara was frazzled.

"I'm feeling drained. I think I'll go home and take a nap." Barbara said, getting up suddenly and heading out of the living room. Terri looked alarmed but understood what she meant, so she walked her to the door.

"Do you want company?"

A cold sweat broke out like grease bubbles on Barbara's forehead.

"Nah, I'll be alright... need some time to think, but thanks. Catch you later."

Barbara boarded the train and headed home. When she arrived, she slumped on the battered leather sofa, like a jigsaw falling into place, and stared at the TV that wasn't on. Her cigarette had burned down to the filter between her stained fingers. Trembling hands quickly lit another. Things started to unravel in Barbara's head, but she had a plan. She called the hospital to arrange for a blood test.

Later that evening, she drove to Alex and Honey-Lee's and watched Honey-Lee prepare for work. Barbara yelled and punched the steering wheel as Honey-Lee reached up in her thousand-dollar Manolo Blahnik heels and kissed Alex full on the mouth before leaving for work. Barbara thought it was like watching a remake of Jaws. She dry-heaved, making an ugly burping sound.

Barbara sat up bone straight when Honey-Lee suddenly appeared in tight, starched whites; she got into the Mercedes Compressor and sped off. That should have been mine, Barbara thought. She followed her, and to her delight, Honey-Lee was none the wiser. She wore red lipstick and seemed to be singing along to something like she was the happiest woman in the world. At the traffic lights, Barbara peered into her bag. Her face, dark and contorted while leaving her house, transformed into a great smile.

"You won't be singing for too long, sweetheart. Enjoy your last song. Go on, sing your heart out... literally!" Barbara burst into giggles as the lights changed to green, and her heart raced as she sped to keep up with Honey-Lee.

Honey-Lee pulled off the road into the Grundy Hospital car park and briskly entered the hospital. She strolled down the coloured stripes on the floor in the corridor, entered a room in the outpatient clinic and began to take tickets from people who wanted to have their blood drawn.

Barbara found a parking space not too far away and entered the hospital. Her smile was even more expansive.

"Not long now."

Her low, sullen tone made the smile a tad eerie. She looked at the red line on the floor in the corridor and imagined it as blood coming from where she had stabbed Honey-Lee in the heart, picturing how she would beg for help while trying to crawl away. Returning to her senses, Barbara snatched a ticket from the machine and joined the end of a very long queue. An older woman with a cheap felt hat was next with the number fifty-eight; Barbara's number was one hundred and six. It was going to be a long wait. Barbara paced rapidly back and forth along the corridor. When it was her turn, she noticed there was no one after her. She looked over her shoulder before entering the room and quietly closed the door.

"H-Hello, are you ready?" Honey-Lee said, taking Barbara's arm.

"Hmmm…yeah… fine," Barbara said, sitting on the edge of a ripped plastic chair.

"Your hands are a bit cold. Can you open and close a few times to increase your circulation," she said, demonstrating the movement. Then Honey-Lee tied a tourniquet around Barbara's upper arm to make the vein stick out. A slick sweat mixed with tears ran down Barbara's face.

Honey-Lee smirked at her in sympathy:

"Are you that scared?"

"Yes, no… it's just…"

"Don't worry, it'll be over before you know it."

"Feeling a bit nauseous…"

"You know what I think about when I need to have an injection? I imagine someone smashing my fingers with a hammer, which soon diminishes the fear of needles. It's a peculiar strategy, I admit, but it works for me. The mental image of something more intense somehow overshadows the anticipation of a simple needle prick." Barbara felt a mixture of nerves and amusement and chuckled at the absurdity of Honey-Lee's coping mechanism. Somebody ate an encyclopedia for dinner, Barbara thought.

Barbara took a deep breath and braced herself for the upcoming injection. Honey-Lee, seemingly unaware of her mental preparation, prepared the syringe with practised ease. Barbara closed her eyes, picturing the imaginary hammer, the sound of smashing echoing in her mind.

Honey-Lee smiled and reached for the butterfly needle. They recommended this usually when patients feared needles, as they looked smaller. Barbara smiled softly, radiantly, then wiped her face with her sleeve. She studied Honey-Lee intently as she prepared the area in the crook of Barbara's elbow. Her heart tap-danced as the temptress searched for the elusive vein. Honey-Lee cleaned the injection site with an alcohol swab and then put the needle into the vein. Barbara winced but strived to be pleasant, even personable. She didn't want to alarm Honey-Lee in any way. It would be a case of mission accomplished within the hour, and then she could let it all out. Barbara's gaze wandered around the room, checking that there were no windows, so no one could see inside the room. The stark white walls seemed to close in, punctuated by posters showcasing anatomical diagrams that she had seen a hundred times before. The sterile scent of disinfectant filled the air, a constant reminder of the clinical setting. Honey-Lee's voice broke through Barbara's momentary distraction, signalling the end of the injection. Her focus shifted back to the task at hand, remembering the pinch, the familiar sensation of the needle piercing her skin. She also reflected on Honey-Lee's professional demeanour. She really couldn't fault her. Barbara drew in a deep breath, her gaze sweeping across the room. The stainless steel surgical instruments, meticulously arranged on the tray, caught her attention, their surfaces gleaming under the fluorescent lights. Forceps, hemostats, trocars, and scalpels formed a precise array. Barbara's eyes lit up upon spotting a syringe. All of a sudden, Honey-Lee blocked her view.

Barbara couldn't believe she had the pleasure of seeing her up so close. She found it hard to believe that Alex's catch of the century was standing in front of her. At the back of Honey-Lee's neck, a few silvery hairs plotted their escape from her scarf. The skin was lined and weathered, almost ruched like a pug's face. Inside, Barbara smiled as she noted how Honey-Lee's uniform strained at the seam down the middle of her back. 'Is this charity shop mannequin better than me?' she thought. Barbara was more determined than ever that Alex would not make such a costly mistake again as long as he lived.

Barbara's gaze lingered on her own arm, now marked by a livid red spot. The injection was over, and a sense of relief washed over her. She took a moment to absorb the details of the room, finding strange comfort in the familiarity of the medical environment. In a matter of seconds, her arm began to throb, which jolted her back to reality, and then came the blood. She had never bled like this before. Honey-Lee dabbed at the area with a ball of cotton. Then she pressed down firmly to stop the bleeding and applied a gauze swab and sticking plaster. Her hands were firm yet so tender, so caring. Despite this, Barbara was adamant that Honey-Lee was guilty as charged because she had the one thing she truly loved. Barbara's hands, which had been white-knuckle clenched and trembling only hours ago, had become super steady and efficient. As Honey-Lee turned away to prepare the blood bottle, Barbara rummaged in her bag, pocketed her mobile, then reached into her own bag and pulled out the syringe. Sweat ran down her forehead and stung her eyes, and she licked the salty moisture that gathered on her top lip. Barbara threw her head back and shrieked:

"Eeeeeeee-yahhhhhhhhh!"

She stabbed Honey-Lee with the needle and smiled from ear to ear, pushing down the plunger. Honey-Lee's eyes grew large in her head, and at first, no words came out. Her mouth opened a few seconds later, and still, nothing came out. Staring, Barbara grinned and waited, still holding on to the plunger.

Honey-Lee threw her head back and howled, and a green vein fit to burst stood out on her temple.

"Want me to call Alex?!" Barbara said, whipping out the syringe.

"Please…" Honey-Lee croaked and slapped a hand over the injection site just before she collapsed to the floor. Barbara checked herself in the mirror before she turned to Honey-Lee.

"Why don't you scream?" Barbara said with lips pulled back from her teeth, "Let's see if you can scream."
Honey-Lee opened her mouth to scream, but nothing came out.

"Try to remember the hammer on fingers thing," Barbara smirked, turning the doorknob.

Choking back tears of relief, she opened the door and left the room. She pushed the hospital doors open, heart pounding, and stepped out into the cool night air. Unseen, the silhouette of the mysterious watcher lingered, a presence cloaked in shadows. The street lamps illuminated the determination-etched lines on Barbara's face as she moved towards the car, the sanctuary awaiting her.

Unlocking the car, she slid into the driver's seat, her hands slightly trembling. A victorious pause hung in the air before she tossed Honey-Lee's mobile phone onto the passenger seat. Barbara's hands gripped the steering wheel, tangible tension coursing through her. The phone buzzed, jolting her focus. Shaky fingers reached for the device, and a furrow creased her brow as she saw Alex's name on the screen. A moment of uncertainty passed before her features softened into a smile, warmth spreading from within.

"Be there soon, my love," she murmured to herself.
The phone buzzed again, and Alex's name flashed on the screen. Barbara wheezed as the weight of her actions pressed against her chest. Her trembling fingers reached for the phone, uncertainty and guilt etched on her face. As she answered, a sinister calm overtook her, and she adopted a composed demeanour.

"Hello?" she spoke, her voice steady despite the pounding heartbeat.

A deep, haunting voice responded on the other end.

"Feel better?"

Chills ran down Barbara's spine as she realised someone was watching, aware of her dark secret. Panic surged, but she masked it with feigned innocence.

"Who are you? Where's Alex? What are you talking about?" she retorted, attempting to sound composed. A low, ominous chuckle echoed through the line.

"I've taken care of Alex for you?"

The unsettling revelation was accompanied by Alex's distant, desperate cries in the background, muffled and fading before falling into an eerie silence.

"But I... but I..." Barbara replied, her voice trembling with fear and confusion.

The Great Rocco

I think I'm toasted… brown bread! I can't see anything. I mean, I really can't see. I hope it ain't the end. Things were getting good for us. If there's a gawd, please save me soul while I tell them what happened, and I promise I'll go straight from here on, cross me heart, and hope to die.

So, there we were, Me and Ronnie. Irish twins, my eye. We weren't even blood. So, don't know why Mum and Uncle Stevo treated us like it. Mum went out of her way to dress us the same, even our hair, for chrissakes. Although younger than Ronnie, being bull-necked from the get-go meant I took charge.

I soon noticed that the more I did for him, the more he bungled me plans, putting spanners in the works or turning up at the wrong time or wrong place. People said he was like it 'cause he wanted to be me or have what I had. On the other hand, I got pure smoke shows, Dom Perignon round the back door, and the whispering Phantom. I had to give him a little something — being the good brother, Jim — so I blessed him with me rejects. Ronnie was a zero, especially when it come to me; he couldn't touch us. But he reckoned he could shine through magic. He wasn't a natural — not by any stretch of the imagination. After studying Muhammad Ali and Rocky one night, he come up with calling himself *The Great Rocco*. How he made the connection is anyone's guess. I mean, come on, Ali and Rocky were epic, but Ronnie was shite, and ya can't even strain piss out of that!

One night, all the kids come round the Dynamo for his show. They all crammed into the front row, eagerly waiting for him. Everyone got a little impatient 'cause he took donkeys. Suddenly, the curtain moved, and out he popped, choking. He stumbled onstage, karate-chopping his way through dry ice. The show hadn't even started, and the kids were bursting all over the place. There wasn't a dry eye in the house. The big lump! Can you imagine all six-bleedin' feet of him swamped in a silver cape and matching tights with a red bulge no thicker than the width of a Mars bar?

Then, entering stage left was his old girl, Mary. A crooked dreg from the Magical Alliance. He didn't like it, but I called her Bloody Mary; there was something about her that I couldn't put me finger on. I reckon she's in her twenties, but something made her seem old like she ate stale food or something, and maybe the crow feathers she stuck in her hair didn't help. Anyway, she crossed the stage in six-inch lizard heels, with cellulite poking through the red fishnets – you know, a bit like when you press cheddar through a grater.

Anyway, she took his cape off and helped him into a straitjacket. The 'nana took a deep breath while she pulled his arms behind his back after tugging Hartley, a baby rabbit's foot, from his hand. After buckling up, she slithered off the stage. Ronnie forgot himself and ogled her fleshy mounds like a lost puppy. I don't know what he see in her. She'd make a bag of onions cry for chrissakes.

As for him and the bleedin' magic tricks, the other night at the ATM, we'd piled the ride with severe reddies. All he had to do was spark the 4x4. We'd all hopped in the getaway to wait for him, and what's he doing? He's holding a book of bleedin' matches, bending one back, flipping it over, bending it this way, and then flicking it with his thumb, but it don't bleedin' light. The alarm sings. I heard the Feds.

I'm like, this ain't the time for magic! I dug in the back, shot out with me propane torch, and whoosh. The 4x4's lit up like Harrod's Christmas tree. He finally got in, and I wedged me foot down, and we got the frig out of there. The boys said to off him, but I told them to hold their horses. He could've really burned us that night.

Anyway, back to the show, Ronnie jerked his arm towards the opposite shoulder and struggled to bring it up over his head. A little girl's mouth dropped open in shock. A few other kids looked at each other as Ronnie undid the sleeve buckle with his teeth.

Can you believe that he wanted to outshine yours truly with this magic-bag-o-bollocks, learning tricks offa YouTube? Me, I wasn't a fan. I only dug magic when Siegfried and Roy's tiger give Roy a love bite of a lifetime. Like Roy, Ronnie sucked big time.

There was this one kid called Billy. Granted, a bit Forest Gump and looks a bit like the Bazooka-Joe kid on the old bubble gum wrappers. He's a funny one, slow but savvy about certain things. He focused so hard on Ronnie as if his life depended on it. As Ronnie's act neared crunch time, he nipped behind his nanny's back.

Meanwhile, Ronnie grunted as he tried to undo the straitjacket's buckles. I swear the kids din't bleedin' blink. Billy shot around Ronnie for a closer look, but his nanny dragged him back to his seat by his collar. He goes utterly ballistic on her, so she give him a sandwich to stick in his pie hole.

As Ronnie made a pig's ear of the straitjacket, he panted like a goodun and continued to struggle. Over the years, I got tired of reminding him to put the stronger arm over the weaker one. I told him over and over about the three-inches-of-slack rule. It was real white-knuckle stuff when he only had twenty seconds to spare. I mean, the kids stared at the clock while he worked himself into a right state. The poor sod didn't know if he was comin' or goin'. From where I was sittin', he was definitely goin' – goin' nuts in his old age. That reminded me to start lookin' for an old fogey's joint.

The 'nana panicked and used the wrong arm, din't he? His mush was proper scarlet. He freed one hand, unzipped, dropped the straitjacket on the floor, and give it:

"YATTAAAAA!"

With the '*trick*' over, Ronnie packed the stuff away, but in haste, he tripped. Little Billy only aimed and lobbed a slice of tomato that splatted on the side of Ronnie's face. The kids went bonkers with explosive laughter.

Then there was the time he put on four sets of handcuffs. That was a right royal faux pas if ever I seen one. I mean, they were legit as hell. He was all Colgate smiling while he showed the audience four sets. He turned his back to them and coated his hands with Vaseline. Then he shouted for Charlie to hold a sheet over them while he magically took them off. One by one, they dropped to the ground, and then, on the last pair, little Billy got loose again, shot over, and yanked the tail of the sheet. He see his nanny on the warpath and kicked over the large tub of Vaseline and then scarpered. Since when did lubrication and being double-jointed become magical? Billy's nanny hunted him down and chased him around the theatre, so he hid behind an old bookshelf. Even Bloody Mary tried to grab him. As she come up, a black feather floated down behind the bookshelf. Billy squeezed in further to get it. The next thing I heard was a gut-wrenching scream that pierced the air. The nanny dragged him out with cut fingers and the feather drenched in blood. On stage, Ronnie pursed his lips to stop his bottom lip from quivering as he carried on, forcing red-raw knuckles through the cuffs. I laughed so hard, me minces were leaking proper, and a snot rocket shot out of me nose.

The following week, after watching Houdini on repeat, he thought he'd have a go. He wrapped himself in a tarpaulin and chained it with a huge padlock. The Great Rocco told the kids to hold their breath as he climbed into a tank that was rapidly filling with water. It just wasn't working out. It got to the point where I really wanted to breathe for the fucker.

The kids' eyes bulged as the water level passed Ronnie's head, and the old chimp blew thousands of bubbles. Mary, pissed on lethal ginger wine and clutching a family-sized bag of Revels, looked concerned yet equally mesmerised by the old boof. The kids hoped he'd make it, but, to be honest, I really didn't

Our running's made us thick and thieves – literally. You see, we proper grafted and had good times before Mary come along. At the end of a bunco, we'd have a jolly at mine, and Ronnie would kick off with one of his tricks. To celebrate an epic jewellery heist, I decided to host a barbeque and invited a few close mates. The air was filled with music, laughter, and chatter. I noticed Ronnie and Mary gazing into each other's eyes as if there was no one else in the world. He's all thumbing the sides of her breasticles. She's moaning and carrying on in me bleedin' kitchen, for chrissakes. She clamped her hand down on his and asked him what we were celebrating. I mean, she wanted him to spill his guts. Ronnie promised to tell her the next day after our meeting. I missed the rest due to the noise. But she didn't let it go; she kept pressing him, pressing him, and the little shit's weak. She reached for his Johnson but accidentally squeezed his rabbit's foot. I had to cover me gob 'cause that's proper funny! She tongues him and clamps down harder on his hand. He's all breathing heavily like Michael friggin' Myers. Then I could tell he was about to give in, so I barged right in there:

"Oi, Oi. Park it, will ya? Ronnie's eyes blink wide open. Mary winks at us, brushes past us, and heads out the door. I shiver like someone walked over me grave.

"She's ya first, an' I get it. But whateva ya do, don't leak our business to Cruella. I've heard she's real bovver."

"Don't be silly, she's cool." Ronnie said.

"Yeah, like lightnin' in a pint of Wray an' Nephew Overproof Rum. When last did ya get ya minces seen to?!"

"Don't say th—"

I'm like, "Ya just balls deep, ain'tcha? Try an' get ya jizz out before ya see 'er next time, so ya mouth don't run."

 Ronnie turned to face me.

"She makes me smile," he said, stroking the rabbit's foot.

"As long as she don't laugh with 'em ol dinghy lips. Suck varnish offa table leg, for gawd's sake!"

"Give her a chance, will ya."

"Ya mean like Billy an' the feather? Don't wanna end up like 'im."

"She likes you and—"

"For the last time, schtum!"

Me and Charlie laugh our heads off as Ronnie did his snake hips number in the middle of the room.

Charlie's like, "See Smithy lurking down the Dynamo the other night. He says Ronnie and Mary's snitches... says we should off 'em ASAP, or we're in for a hot spell at Queenie's pleasure. Told him I'd run it by ya."

"What?"

"He spot Ronnie and the sea donkey hot-footin' it out the copshop in Bethnal Green."

"He'd never."

"Ya betta get someone to take care of it, or Smithy will."

I rub me face with both hands.

"Don't want Smithy to take 'im out. That's too cold. "I know Ronnie's dumber than a set of boulders, but he's like a real brother to me."

"You can't say I never told ya!"

I shouted at Ronnie, "Ya got some nerve... polishin' ya roach-killers on me fifty gran' Isfahan an' callin' it bleedin' dancin'."

 Charlie giggled.

"The doctor says my heart's gettin' stronger. I'll visit you in Scrubs. I'll even bring soap. Nudge, nudge, wink, wink.

I just stared him down.

"You'd be with us too, ya plonker."

I pretended to be a sniper, drawing a bead on Ronnie's head. I pointed a finger at him and went, BOOM!

"A snitch is a terrible thing!"

*****

Dreamers say love'll make you do funny things. Ronnie didn't just fall in love; he dove in with concrete blocks attached to both feet. Why anyone would want to fall is a great conundrum, but he did, and that was the problem. Every time we did a number, it was Mary wants, Mary needs, Mary says—all the time. Bloody Mary! Well, it was getting old, especially after the Hatton number.

Ronnie even put magic on the back burner when it come to her. They were always vibratin', if you catch me drift. He'd never had it so good. They were addicted to each other. It was just a matter of time before he spilt. Ya see, with her, his mouth knew no bounds; it forever leaked our business. It needed a new washer, and as luck would have it, I had a rep for changing them. Now, as I mentioned earlier about love, yes, I had a kind of love for the horror show, but over the years, I'd learned that dumb is dumb, no matter how ya cut it. Also, love aside, I was too long in the tooth for a lengthy spell at Her Majesty's.

That Saturday night, he come to see me all rather odd, as they'd normally be out on the razz. His pants were flyin' so high that his socks took all the credit. Nervous sweat dripped down his face, and he was all tied at tongue 'cause he knew I was his black dog. The lump had that doltish smile plastered on his face as he stroked the clingfilm over a tattoo of a 40s pinup girl with Bloody Mary's face. I scratched my head as I didn't know what to make of it. He proudly explained each detail, how the pinup girl's wink mirrored Bloody Mary's mischievousness. As he rambled on, I couldn't help but wonder if he'd lost his four marbles.

"I'm finished with the business," he said, not even looking at us. I just pulled on me fag and kept me other hand on the gun in me pocket. I moved to the edge of me seat and slapped me palm on the table.

"What're ya yakkin' about? Ya gone soft? I'm the one to tell ya when it's outs!"

"It's time for me and—" he said.

"If it weren't for us, ya would've been a nillionaire shovelling pig shit!"

"You can say what you like, Jim, b-but I'm out." He closed his eyes and slowly exhaled.

I looked over his shoulder at Bloody Mary's face on the tattoo. It's like she had her hand up his backside, telling him what to say and do.

"She got her hand up ya jacksie, has she?"
He just stared at the floor, all sweated up, reeking onions. I knew it was bite time.

"S-she's... my happily ever after... with my cut of the money... she wants us to live in Charleston Manor."

I could feel the lines in me forehead gagging for polyfiller.

"Ow many times' ave I warned ya 'bout leakin' our business?"

"Erm... she thinks we... I s-should have a bigger cut bec—"
I grit me teeth in silent fury.

"Bigger cut, me bleedin' eye! Shut ya gob. That's what ya need a bigger cut of. Ya want me to stick a washer on it for ya? Is that whatcha want?"

I shot to the window and felt the gun, nice and cool in me pocket.

"Bloody Mary this, Bloody Mary that... all the time, Bloody Mary..."

For a moment, Ronnie turned to watch us, then went back to stroking the cling film. Every time I looked at the bleedin' tattoo, I could have sworn it was bleedin' movin'.

He don't look up. "Y-you can't stop us," he whispered.
I fingered the bullets, slipping them out and feeding them into the chamber, all while looking out the window. Once fully loaded, I held the gun in me hand, feeling the coolness ooze up me arm. Slowly, I walked around the back of his chair. He smoothed the cling film's edges as he waltzed through a mental list of things to say to us.

"She's got in-the-bedroom-eyes."

I'm like, "More like bleedin' piss holes in the snow."

"Didn't know they could make tattoos... so real, like. Did you, Jimbo?"
I didn't really know if I could do it. I stared at the back of his neck. Me hands shook as I weighed things up. I raised the gun but couldn't bring meself to do it.

"Erm... Did ya... speak ta Feds?"

"Who, me? Nah." Ronnie winced, trembled, and pursed his lips to keep his teeth from chattering. "And you know what? We're gonna go on that cruise... and after... I'll have a Vegas-style comeback." Burning white rage filled me eyes. I fingered the barrel, no major hurry. Then, time sped up, and within a minute, I stood in front of Ronnie, closed me eyes, and squeezed the trigger.
BANG!

A single, hurt shot to the head. Ronnie's eyes opened real wide, then rolled back. Glistening crimson splattered everywhere. He gargled and spluttered as he spilled out of the chair, slumping to the floor.

Brain and blobs decorated me shirt, trousers, and the skirting boards. "Brains are made up of 12 per cent fat. If it dries, it's gonna shag me Louboutins."

I got on me knees and stared at him.

"God looks after babies and fools, eh? He'll take care of ya, alright." I gawped while blood trickled from the corner of his eye. The old soak bled out on me bleedin' Isfahan. As I checked his pulse, the reality sunk in that I'd done him.

I hadn't planned it like that, but to be honest, not only had I carried him since the devil was a boy, but I had to worry about Bloody Mary's meddling, too. Straw and camel's back is all I'm saying. When he hit the floor, the cling film rolled back, showing the tattoo's bold colours—quite incredible artwork for a poxy studio in Peckham.

Mission accomplished, methinks. Whistling in appreciation, I placed the .38 right up against Bloody Mary's eye. Me nostrils flared as I pulled the trigger.

BANG!

"Goodnight, Ronnie. Buh-bye, Bloody Mary. We'll meet again; don't know where, don't know when." I cracked up at the ragged hole in his arm.

Pacing like no one's business, I spat rapid-fire instructions for Charlie to get the van, kit, barrel, and boat. But he wanted none of it. I reminded him that we're all dirty fingers in the Hatton job. He's all wheezing down the blower, telling me he's gonna have a heart attack. I thought it was funny how he didn't complain when we were stacking reddies on the ATM job. Then I chain-smoked like Thomas the friggin' Tank Engine, looking out the bleedin' window for the bugger. I swear to no lie; when I looked through the window, I see a reflection that wasn't mine for chrissakes. It's bleedin' Ronnie's! I jumped and slammed the window shut. Then, I thought someone was in the room. The door slammed shut, and I swivelled around, expecting to see Charlie. But there was no Charlie. For a minute, I thought it was Ronnie. So, I ran back to him. I mean, I checked his pulse and everything to be sure he was dead.

"Ron, it's Jimbo," I said softly, talking to the dead fart. For the first time in me life, I felt for the git.

"S-s-sorry, bro, but it had to be—"

A sudden pounding on the door startled the fuck out of me. I got to me plates of meat real quick! I lifted me hand to open the door but stopped meself just in time and pressed me eye to the peephole.

I couldn't believe me eyes; it was Bloody Mary. She's all hands on hips, waiting for us to open up. I just prayed that Charlie didn't turn up. I stood there, pulling on me fag, and waited. After a few minutes, her footsteps clattered away. I ran to the window to see her jump into a black car and take off. Not long after, there was another pounding on the door. Thank gawd it was Charlie. I was so relieved, but he could only scowl as I dragged him in sharpish and shut the door. I flew him up the stairs without a word. In silence, we both stared at Ronnie and then at each other.

"Y-ya... did 'im?" he said.

"C'mon, get ya finger out!" Charlie gawped at us like he'd seen bird poo on a Krispy Kreme donut.

"He's ready for the fishies. Was in cahoots with feds, for gawd's sake!"

"Where we gonna put him?" Charlie traipsed towards me, shock pinching his already pinched rat-face.

"Always bangin' on about cruises, so gonna give 'im a noble sea burial. C'mon!"

We wrapped Ronnie's body in the Isfahan and lugged it down to the kitchen. On the way, Ronnie's head bumped the bannisters.

I was like, "Watch' is bleedin' nut, will ya."

"He's hardly gonna feel—"

Cocking me finger like a gun, I pointed at Charlie.

"Ya wanna cruise with 'im?"

***

We rolled the body onto plastic sheeting. Charlie bunched up the Isfahan, chucked it into the van, and brought in a pathetically small crate.

"A bleedin' crate, for gawd's sake? Where's the rest? He's grown, not eight! Wassup with the drum?"

"I-I-I—"

I opened the kit and had a rummage.

"Charlie, there's no bleedin' acid in 'ere. Ya forgot the bleedin' acid, too."

Charlie heaved the crate on top of the plastic. We both studied it, then looked at Ronnie.

"Is he gonna fit?"

"Do I look like Mystic Meg?"

I grabbed me Bowie. Growling and baring me teeth, I scored Ronnie's wrist. Jabbing the knife in, it got stopped by bone. I prodded, and the tip snapped.

At that point, I spat feathers.

"What the 'eck am I gonna do now?"

Charlie pointed to the kit.

"Saw's in there."

"Damn, weren't even plannin' a bleedin' carvery."

Still dazed, Charlie ran to the kit, got the saw, and passed it to us. I hacked into Ronnie's arm, and Charlie gagged as it sliced through the tatted arm joint. I'm a man on a mission as I go at it! Sweat dripped from me bald patch, past me barnet spears, and down me neck. After a vicious snap, I twisted his arm off, and it hit the plastic with a dull thud. A stunned Charlie looked on and shook like nobody's business. Tense, he kneeled.

"Saw blade's gunked."

"Blimey O' Reilly!"

I gritted me teeth and cleaned the blade. I had to blink sweat from me eyes before attacking another limb. Charlie watched, his face an ashy mess.

I grinned.

"Just think of... a quality Chateaubriand."

"Chat. What? Gonna be—" Charlie said. He shot to the bathroom, leaving bloody footprints. When finished sprogging me deed, he come back.

When it was all over, we tried lifting Ronnie, but talk about dead weight. We cocked the crate and shoved him in until he stacked up nicely. I chucked the Bloody Mary arm on top, and Charlie popped the lid on.

Charlie hammered so many nails into the crate that I had to grab his arm to make him stop. While he went to check if there was no one around, I had a fag. When he come back, I stubbed me fag, and we set to heaving the crate out the side door, down the alley to the van. As I stepped out behind Charlie, he turned around paler than the moon; you would have thought he'd seen a ghost.

*****

On the way to East Jesus, neither of us said boo. The crate banged against the sides in the back. Charlie drove like there was a fog on. He was all perched on the edge of his seat, knuckles white and eyes on stalks. It was dead of night and pitch black when we finally arrived, but for the moon. We tugged the crate out and dragged it to shore. The combination of night air and raw sea might have been thought romantic at any other time, but not on this occasion. The waves crashed and tumbled. The tide come in and out, and me heart drummed as I waited for Charlie and the boat. After about twenty minutes, he come, head down, hauling it. Me heart did one when he flopped face-first into the sand and then struggled for donkeys to get up. I couldn't believe me eyes. I mean, ya just couldn't make it up.

We tried to get the crate in the boat for ages, but it was no mean feat. Finally, after a mega heave, it thudded in, causing a crack in the bottom. Pushing the boat past the water's edge, we clambered in and rowed. Charlie's chest hurt and he wanted to go home, but I wouldn't hear it. With a rush of adrenaline, heart racing – the lot, we chanced choppy waters.

As we sailed further out, the moon became judge and jury to our shenanigans. Water sloshed underfoot, and that's when I realised Ronnie'd jacked me plans yet again. Climbing on the bench was the safest bet, but it snapped, and me foot almost skidded through the crack. Charlie yanked me up. We trembled on the edge, trying to keep our balance.

Suddenly, what looked like Ronnie's ghost rose out of the crate, choking violently. The rabbit's foot flew out of its mouth and hit me smack in the chest. Well, me and Charlie screamed like little girls. I scooted back on me heels and grabbed onto Charlie as we both struggled to get away.

"What the…?"

"I told ya… I told ya. I'm The Great Rocco, and I'm gonna show ya how great I really am!" said Ronnie's ghost.

"Don't ya come near me!"

"God takes care of babies and fools, eh? Well, we'll see who's the fool." He laughed like a proper maniac.

"Yattaaaaaaa!"

The wind howled, and a lightning bolt struck as the heavens rumbled and roared. Waves reared up, collapsed, crashed, and spilled. Ronnie's ghostly hand clamped down on me throat, shaking us like a bleedin' leaf.

"You like gifts, don't you? Well, I got you a little keepsake for your birthday," said Ronnie's ghost.

That's all I 'member before I blacked out. It was the howling wind that brought us round again.

"Get up, we've gotta move," Charlie shouted.

Attacked by vicious winds, we pushed on further out into churning waves. We bent against the waves, against terror, as we fought like hell to get the crate out of the boat before it sunk the lot of us. The boat rocked and shuddered with each wave, but we gritted our teeth and clung to the crate, muscles straining. Every desperate heave against the waves brought us closer to either victory or defeat.

"There's water in the boat. Get him out. Get him out, Charlie!"
He's all shooketh while I crawled to the other end of the boat.

"Oh, for gawd's sake, me Loubs!"
Charlie put his arms around me chest and hoiked me up. We both
sat on the edge, as far away as we could from Ronnie's crate.
Charlie clutched his chest.

"Ca—n't."

"It's not much further. Please, Charlie, me old mate!"

We rowed like the clappers, and our faces lit up every now and
then from the lightning bolts. The sky rumbled overhead, then a
loud thunderclap.

BOOM!

An epic slap from a wave tilted the boat, smacking it down into the
water. We all got tossed out into the sea, and Ronnie's crate bobbed
in the distance. Then I nearly lost it 'cause me head went under at
one point, and when I come up, it was like the crate was treading
water right next to us. I didn't realise how far out we were. We had
to move in rocket fashion to get back to shore.

A flash of lightning showed Charlie's thrashing body, arms, and
legs bombing it to shore. I tried to catch up, but it was like Michael
Phelps had possessed the git. By the time I thought about it,
something had slapped me in the face, and then I got dragged
under.

"Wait up, Phelpsy!"

I got proper rag-dolled by the waves, and massive tangles of
seaweed grabbed at us. I kicked and fought to keep from going
under. I turned and saw the top of the crate. Again, it seemed
closer. As I neared the edge, me feet tangled in something; it felt
like hands grabbing me ankles. I scrapped like a goodun to get 'em
loose. Panic surged as the slippery strands wrapped around me
ankles, threatenin' to pull us under. With a mix of fear an'
determination, I wriggled and twisted, managin' to free one foot,
then the other.

Suddenly, the moon disappeared, and it was eerie and proper calm. I crawled to shore, spluttering, a gasping wreck. Getting nearer, Charlie was lying with his hand on his heart.

"Oi, Charlie, ya all right?"

He struggled to breathe and whimpered.

"It's my heart, Jim!" He sat up, groaning.

Out the corner of me eye, something moved.

"Ya see that?"

"What?" Charlie said, turning around.

"Someone's watching."

Adrenalin had me going like a young 'un, but I stopped when me knees only popped and cracked. I plodded to the end of the pier, and that's when I saw a flash of light by the car park. Tyres screeched, and a black car pulled away. I'm sure it was her, Mary, Bloody Mary. After about five minutes, out of puff, I went back for Charlie.
He panted. "Who was it?"

"Me gut says Bloody Mary."

"You sure?"

"A hundred, mate. We've got to sort her, too, now."

"Please, Jim, not tonight."

*****

After I dropped Charlie, I bombed it back to have Courvoisier and fag to thaw out. I had just taken a gulp when someone pounded on the door. I rushed to the peephole, thinking Charlie had come back for something; I opened the door and nearly swallowed me tongue when I see Bloody Mary with accusing eyes.

"Well, invite me in!"

She breezed in like she owned the joint. As she strutted down the corridor, she glanced in me rooms as if she expected to see Ronnie. After gettin' to me living room, she sat on the edge of the seat with her fat ass and bubblegum legs. The mare was killing me favourite chair, then she sobbed like a six-year-old girl who dropped her ice cream.

I mean, she shook like there was some kind of inner earthquake going on. I gave her a box of tissues, and then her weepy eyes scanned the room like she lost something.

"So, what happened?"

I forced tears, then pretended to wipe me eyes.

"Well, like I said, Ron just up and left... told us... about... erm, some cruise..."

I watched her shrewdly and, again, saw a flicker of disbelief in her eyes. I kept staring as she turned an angry shade of red.

"Cruise... our cruise. But why'd he go without me?"

I ran me fingers over me head and shrugged me shoulders, but I wanted to take me fag and out it on her eyeballs.

Bloody Mary mopped at tears and sniffled.

"What am I going to do?"

I rolled me eyes to the ceiling.

"He always wanted to travel the world and share his gift of magic."

Bloody Mary sobbed. She stood up and stared at me square in the face. I can't quite explain what happened, but I was mesmerised by the contrast of the crow feathers in her hair and breasticles like full-moon-white-orbs. She looked white... a luminous white, like she'd light up the darkest room, white. I don't know what come over us; I couldn't turn me head away. The only thing that wasn't white was her teeth; they were striking for a different reason, and that's because they were yellow. To be precise, it would be a Cigarette Stain Yellow on the Dulux paint chart. As I had it out with me thoughts, her eyes narrowed, and then, with the battle cry of Satan, she lunged and slapped me face so hard me head wobbled. Then, she give us the death stare.

"Don't you... Don't you even... You... you lying piece of crap. I know what you fuckers did."

"Even what?"

"You really want me to spell it out?"

"Spell what?"

Then the sea-donkey started to laugh, a laugh that for a moment actually made the hairs on the back of me neck bristle.

I raised me hand to me cheek; I didn't know what to do.

"Out. Now. If ya value ya life, git the fuck!"

Grabbing hold of her, I jostled her out of me house and into the street. I slammed the door, leaned against it, and breathed heavily. I heard her losing her marbles outside.

"I'm gonna fix you. If it's the last thing I do."

Then there was a deep, gut-wrenching wail like a lost, frightened child.

"Roc… co… Roc…co!"

I locked the door and grabbed me glass, knocking back the Courvoisier. Me eyes darted around the room to check that I hadn't forgotten any of Ronnie's leftovers. I sighed with relief when I couldn't see any. But under the bleedin' chair, me eyes zoomed in on a black crow feather. Tremblin' with pure shock, I gulped. I clenched me hands in front of me face with me elbows on the table.

I knew Charlie would be as useful as a sponge in the sea, so I had to take care of it. Later that day, I waited in the car outside the Magical Alliance. When Bloody Mary finally come out, the streets were empty. She turned, spotted me ride, and took to her heels like Redrum. I revved the engine, mounted the pavement, and plowed into her. She screamed; she had no chance. Not one.

*****

The following week, I split Ronnie's portion of the Hatton heist with Charlie. We celebrated with a magnum of champagne. Charlie chucked in brown sugar cubes and Angostura bitters and filled our flutes to the brim.

"Ahem. You seen 'im?" Charlie said.

"Nah, thank gawd!"

We giggled and emptied our flutes like we were drinking Coca-Cola on a hot summer's day.

"When do you wanna deal with the sea donkey?"

"Done and dutifully dusted, my friend."

"What? You did it?"

"Yeah, the binmen should be taking it to the dump about now."

"Shit, Jim! For real? What now?"

"Onwards and upwards, right? We can have whatever we want."

"Yeah, whispering Rolls Royce's on its way."

I admired the glint from the triangular diamond in me pinky ring.

"So, erm, what exactly happened to the sea... Mary?"

"I guess you could call it a accident."

"What happened?!"

"Well, hmmm... after I dropped ya, she come by giving it large, and I sent her packing. She shot out of that magic joint and didn't look where she was going. Then, she clocked us and turned all Redrum. It was too late for us to hit the brakes, and I just give her a little tap with me bumper."

"Tap?" Charlie said.

"Yeah, the bumper got the worst of it, though." I said, examining me pinky diamond. "Such a sad state of affairs."

Charlie shook his head from side to side. "Life, eh?"

"What can ya do?"

"Here, Charleston Manor's still up for sale." Charlie jabbed a finger on the picture in Homes and Property magazine.

I was gassed. "What? Ronnie and Bloody Mary's gaff?"

"Got a bad feeling about it, Jimbo!"

"Can't see why not. It's not like they're gonna put in an offer, is it?"

I snatched the magazine out of Charlie's hand and checked the date. I ripped the page out and examined the details. Then I got on the blower to the estate agent, and the Hooray Henry told me that some boujee bitch was determined to buy the property.

I told him to tell her to sling her hook. He defended, but I reminded him that cash was king, and I was good for it. In a matter of days, I did the business and signed all the necessary documents. I couldn't wait to dig my claws into it.

*****

When the day come, I hit a button on the automatic remote control and beamed like Batman's Joker as the wrought iron gates swung open, revealing grounds that sprawled out forever in front of us.

I stared at Charlie.

"Welcome to Buckham House. Happy Bornday to me and all that!"

"You bought it? You never!"

"Now, that's what ya call bleedin' magic," I said, clouting him on the back. Then we had a good giggle.

"Ya sneaky... son-of-a-gun!"

I roared with laughter.

"Nah, I'll settle for Lord Muckety-Muck, actually."

*****

A few months later, it became a running joke about me being king of the castle. Charleston Manor was terrific, and everyone thought so. Me and Charlie discovered a selection of unlimited Moulin De La Lagun in the cellar. Me dos at the weekend went well beyond noon the next day. I even bought a round table to display the cellar's varied gems. We also found countless barrels behind a screen down there. One Friday evening, curiosity got the better of us, and I decided to find out what they contained. After all, I'd been lucky with the wine; maybe it'd be the same.

Anyway, I picked one, turned the tap, put me glass under, and watched it fill with a dark ruby liquid. I sipped, noting the delicate but rich, silky texture.

I told Charlie to investigate, and he contacted Lanneau, who told us about Noval Nacional 1963. The other Kardashian-assed barrel was definitely vintage – something about En Primeur. Lanneau bottled the liquid and took it for authentication. I couldn't wait for the results. I didn't understand all that French malarkey, but something told me I'd hit the jackpot.

Overjoyed, I unearthed many similar barrels, so we drained them at the parties. One day, we pulled out a barrel we'd been drinking from and realised it should've been empty but wasn't. We were puzzled. After all, it was far heavier than it should've been. We flicked on the light and pulled it down. As it straightened, liquid trickled on the floor. I put me finger in and tasted. Then Charlie did, too. We stared at each other and roared with laughter.

Charlie chiselled off the lid; I took the torch and looked inside but couldn't see the bottom. There was a dribble, but it felt like more was in there. Maybe a stash of something. Charlie had the same idea, and both, really fired up about the find, decided to cave it with the hammer. As he chopped, bits of wood, liquid, and sweat beads flew. Some of the sides splintered and lay on the floor, but other than that, the thing wouldn't give. Moments later, I took over and had a go. Exhausted, I propped up the wall while Charlie explored with the torch. With a stunned look on his face, he was all croaky, choking on his words as if he got booted in the gut. He staggered away from the barrel.

"What?" I said.

"It can't be… can it?" Charlie gripped the bench like his life depended on it. "Shit," he said, and then I thought he was bloody stroking.

"Oh, for Jesus, please say it ain't. Jim. We gotta get out of here…"

Charlie's legs went, and he slunk to the floor.

I froze, stunned. "What're you on about?"

Charlie really looked like he'd swallowed a snake.

I snatched the torch, pointed, and inched to the barrel. Something strange-looking and colourful glistened. I jumped back – almost out of me skin. The torch slipped from me hand. When I finally got it together, I picked it up and crawled to the side of the barrel. What was left of Ronnie's water-logged face was caked in blood. His smile was horrid, with a black tongue sticking out the side of his mouth. Blood shot to me head, and black spots bounced before me eyes. Me and Charlie raced to the stairs, and the bleedin' light went out as we hit the first step. From somewhere, we heard Bloody Mary laughing hysterically. Well, I budged Charlie out of the way, and we flew up the stairs to the kitchen as if in the business of breaking records. Bloody Mary's laughter got louder still. Charlie slammed the door shut and bolted it.

In the kitchen, we chugged Courvoisier 'til it dribbled down our chins. Minutes later, the doorbell rang. I got up and peeped before I opened the door. There was no one there. Looking down, I saw Lanneau's box.

At last, something to take the sting out of the 'mare. I brought it inside and set it on the table. It was a pine box with 'Happy Birthday' in red paint along the side. Charlie opened it and stared at the contents with his mouth open in shock.

Inside was Ronnie's arm with the tattoo of a winking Bloody Mary lying on a bed of straw. Well, Charlie clutched his chest, keeled over, and hit the deck. Shaking like I had buck fever, I checked his pulse. He'd croaked alright. There was somethin' in the envelope. Eagerly, I squeezed it. A cloud of some stinkin' gas filled the air. I took out the hand-scrawled note that read:

'With best compliments, Ronnie & Mary'
As I fought for each breath, the note slipped from my trembling fingers, my throat feeling tight, as if invisible hands were strangling me.

Coming soon… **BLACKBALLED**.
This Deliciously Dark Short Story collection features five tales of subtle terror, each with a unique twist. The stories unfold with a diverse cast of characters, all driven by a penchant for pushing boundaries. It's a tailor-made collection that is best enjoyed during the daylight hours!

The first story, '**Blackballed**,' introduces an arrogant pool player who meets his match in the form of two teenage girls on a mission to teach him a lesson on how to *really* play. From there, we delve into '**86,**' following the protagonist as she navigates the intriguing world of a Thai massage parlour with a unique menu featuring numbered massages. When she encounters the number 86, an unexpected twist unfolds. Next is the spooky tale '**Deja Brew**,' where a pensioner becomes convinced his wife is having an affair, unaware that her lover departed long ago. In '**Twisted**,' we peer through the eyes of a husband seeking to rekindle his youth when he encounters an old-school flame at a wedding. The collection concludes with '**La Oubliette Noir**,' tackling themes of revenge and justice as those who escape the law finally receive their just desserts.

Read the captivating first part of '**Blackballed**' and discover the chilling ending awaiting you in the rest of the collection.

BLACKBALLED
M. HENNINGHAM

Blackballed

Brad and Patsy argued all evening after he leered at Jan in her old-style waitress's uniform and fishnet stockings at the barbecue. Patsy even noticed him licking his lips and staring at her in the rear-view mirror. Brad thought she didn't know, that she couldn't tell. After dropping Jan off at home, they had a confrontation in the street because he denied it. Sulking, he suggested they go home too, but she knew it would end badly. She looked at him with bloodshot eyes and told him she wanted to play pool, as she couldn't bear the thought of him harassing her for sex.

When they arrived at the pool hall, he parked outside. Upon entering, Brad scanned the room for the best table and paid. Stuffing a bulging wallet into his back pocket, he threw his keys at Patsy, and she placed them in her bag. With chalk and balls in one hand and drinks in the other, he spotted two girls a few tables away, one with a pony hawk and the other with a bob cut. He beamed from ear to ear. Brad loved an audience, especially young females. After chalking his cue and racking the balls, he theatrically rolled up the sleeves of an imaginary shirt.

An explosive crack sent the balls spinning all over the table. A coloured one slid into a side pocket. Brad bent to check before sinking another. Patsy scowled as he paced around the table, his spindly legs fuelled by enthusiasm. She visualised conking him on the forehead with the white ball to teach him a lesson.

Brad positioned himself with one foot on the floor and the other hanging off the table. Then he stepped back and frowned – using the cue to work out the angles, which Patsy found annoying. She knew he only did it for the sake of his prepubescent fans. Brad pulled the cue back but hesitated. Finally, he pulled back the cue again and struck the ball, then potted the first, the second, the third, and the fourth.

"Can you believe it?" he said, chalking the cue. Then, he missed the next shot. Patsy smirked, and her face turned a bit red. She started sweating and sat at the table, blotting with tissue. Then she took a swig of Southern Comfort and Red Bull, but it didn't seem to be working; it only enhanced the rage, causing her to miss the cue ball on her next shot. Brad stifled giggles, but she thanked God under her breath when he missed his shot. When it was her turn, she stepped up to the table all business-like, trying to make up for lost ground. She potted one, then another. In a few minutes, the tide turned, and she made a series of impressive fluky shots but acted as though they were intended. While she was on a roll, Brad looked red and mad as hell. From the corner of her eye, Patsy could see his brain working, figuring out a way to foil her.

He said, "What you wanna do after—"

"Stop trying to put me off!" Patsy snapped, gripping the cue.

Then, it was all down to the black ball. She walked around, trying to figure out the best angle. Patsy rested the cue on top of her shaky hand. At the same time, one of the other pool players responded to a goal on the widescreen television.

"One nil!"

Patsy jumped; her shot rebounded off the cushion and veered away from the pocket. Suddenly, Brad snatched his cue and chalked it, concentrating with his tongue sticking out to the side. After examining the tip, he positioned himself on the table, pulled back the cue, and sank the black ball.

Pony Hawk and Bob Cut cheered for him. Patsy cast a sharp glance their way and slammed her glass down on the table. Brad breezed around the pool table, glancing at the girls and flexing his biceps. When Pony Hawk winked at him, he met her gaze and reciprocated. At the same time, Bob Cut rolled her eyes towards the ceiling.

It was just after 9 pm when Patsy had had enough and wanted to go home. She could not deal with the flirting anymore. She told Brad she'd wait in the car for five minutes, and if he didn't come, he'd find her at home. It was either that or stay and serve him the cue in a very unnatural way and force a couple of stripes down his throat. Instead of going with her, he raised the stakes he would not be able to come back from. The girls watched intently, their smothered giggles drifting across the hall. As Patsy stormed out, Pony Hawk and Bob Cut eyed the door, checking to see if she'd really gone. After a while, they saw her speed off and moved in for the real game.

Brad took out a pound coin and rammed it into the slot. The balls clunked down into the mechanism under the table. Brad peered at Pony Hawk.

"Want Big Daddy to teach you some tricks, sexy?"

"I'm not very good," she smiled, glancing at Bob Cut, who rolled her eyes to the ceiling.

Brad licked his lips. "I'm sure I can teach you a thing or three."

Checking her out as she bent over the table, he moved in behind to guide her shot. She pressed backwards into him. Brad stood firm and didn't move. Minutes passed; he moved to the side, showing her how to make a bridge with her hand. After encouraging her to look down the cue as if holding a bow and arrow, she returned to her table and whispered something to Bob Cut. Again, Brad stared at Pony Hawk and winked. Then, after a slight pause, he reached beneath the table for the triangle. He racked up, placing stripes and spots correctly before positioning the black ball. He concentrated, tongue out to the side while he twisted the chalk on the end of his cue. Little did he know that it would be the last time he would twist anything, as an unexpected turn of events lurked just around the corner...

Other books by M. Henningham

Welcome to a world where each tale is a whisper that beckons you into the depths of the unknown. This enigmatic collection, born from the shadows of inspiration, unveils itself with a series of stories that will leave your senses tingling and your mind craving more. The journey begins with **'Soulless,'** a gripping narrative that follows a young woman's desperate quest to break free from the clutches of a relentless stalker. The inspiration for this tale was drawn from the haunting echoes of real-life stories of resilience and survival. As you venture further into the heart of darkness, **'Delusion 13'** awaits, a thrilling tale that ensnares a luckless man who believes he has discovered the woman of his dreams. Feel the city's pulse in **'Shootin' Candy,'** a tale that dives into the themes of power and greed. This story thrusts a privileged teen past the point of no return, where morality hangs in the balance and the dark side of the tracks beckons. **'Tell Him to Run'** unfolds as a poignant exploration of choices born from desperation and poverty. The inspiration for this tale was ignited by the indomitable spirit of those facing insurmountable odds. **'Behaving Badly'** delves into the psyche of an unstable young man fiercely protective of his parents. This chilling narrative explores the lengths one can go to ensure the safety of those they love. Brace yourself for a journey where the shadows hold secrets that will leave you questioning the boundaries between darkness and light.

REVIEW

MASTERFUL SHORT STORIES

This is one of the best short story collections I've ever read. I can say with all honesty that no matter what genre of work you prefer, you will miss out on some of the edgiest and best writing a reader can devour. There are five (would have eaten far more) tales of victims and perpetrators that are delivered from first person point of view. Normally, this might, in a short story, result in a thinly painted descriptive monologue, but the authors commanding style of writing delivers. You will enter the dark and often seedy world of the protagonists, you will feel their pain, frustration and fear. There are deeper messages in each of the stories, thought provoking understanding of the circumstances that cause us or the characters to behave badly, even an innocent child manifesting fears by reading the emotional undercurrents between loving and caring parents. This is definitely a must read. I am now going to work my way through the other books published by this author.

Coming soon...

Honeydickers follows the daring exploits of three teenage grifters whose livelihood depends on the art of the steal. Their latest caper involves duping a detestable store owner in the depths of Hatton Garden, but little do they realise the gravity of their actions. News of their heist reaches the ears of a vengeful pursuer, propelling the trio to seek refuge in the sun-soaked escapism of Ibiza.

However, their quest for redemption turns sinister when they encounter a macabre, godlike figure lurking in the shadows. Undeterred by the supernatural aura surrounding this enigmatic being, the teens hatch a plan to rip him off, only to find themselves entangled in a web of divine wisdom.

As destinies collide and the thin line between justice, rebellion, and divine darkness blurs, chaos becomes the only constant. What unforeseen perils await these young grifters in this twisted dance of fate?